Love My Enemy

Love My Enemy

Kate MacLachlan

Andersen Press • London

For Ian, James, Linnhe and Darroch

O5522944

First published in 2004 by
Andersen Press Limited,
20 Vauxhall Bridge Road, London SWIV 2SA
www.andersenpress.co.uk

Reprinted 2005

British Library Cataloguing in Publication Data available

ISBN 1 84270 340 4

Typeset by FiSH Books, London WC1
Printed and bound in Great Britain by Mackays of Chatham Ltd.,
Chatham, Kent

1

'Fantastic – it's peeing!'

Zee, mortified, prayed for a small bomb, but the twins were screaming with delight. They grabbed each other's hands and whirled around, faster and faster, a dizzying kaleidoscope of thin limbs and flying gravel, until physics intervened and sent them spinning, in opposite directions, to the ground.

'Ouch!'

'Would you look at that?' said their mother, Sue, in disbelief. 'I've actually done it – it works!'

'Most kits work,' said Zee cuttingly.

'Oh, love, I know you weren't keen, but don't you think it's cute now it's up and running?'

'Up and peeing, you mean.' Zee surveyed the two-foot stone statue in dismay. 'I think it's gross, Mum, downright tacky. Couldn't you at least have picked one with water coming out of his *mouth*?'

'We wanted this one,' declared Josh, staggering as he achieved vertical.

'Yeah, he's got curly hair like us,' said Gemma.

'Hardly his most striking feature.' Zee's lip curled in distaste. 'Heaven knows what the new neighbours will think. I bet they heard this was a classy area.' She glanced, for the hundredth time, at the big removal van parked a few yards down the street. *Rutters English*

1

Carriers was emblazoned in two-foot high letters on the side. 'And I bet *their* choices aren't made by six-year-olds.'

Her mother side-stepped the accusation. 'There's just one child I believe – about your age – according to Mrs Gordon. The father's foreign, a musician.'

Zee shrugged. It seemed very uncool to be interested in anything their nosy neighbour, Mrs Gordon, said but in fact, local gossip was the only reason she was hanging out in the garden. Her mum spent hours here, whole days sometimes; planting, pruning, feeding, thinning. Why, Zee often wondered? What was the point of it all?

After three hours Zee feared that her body might start to self-destruct with boredom. Much earlier, a silver Renault had pulled into the garage of Number 2 Hazel Grove. Zee had legged it up the laburnum tree – for some peace she claimed – just in time to see a black-haired man, a slim woman and a girl in jeans vanish inside the big house on the corner.

She had been waiting for the girl to reappear ever since. This had meant heaving stones about at her mother's request and shovelling tons of gravel in around the grotesque little water feature. She had handled spiky plants which would look more at home in a tropical jungle, and spent hours squeezing kinks out of an old hose with more holes in it than the *Titanic*. In all that time nobody interesting had shown up – not even cute Conor from Number 9.

'They've got some nice furniture,' said her mum, nodding towards the van. 'Look at that chaise longue.'

'Let's go and say hello,' cried Gemma.

'Not now, love, they'll be busy. Plenty of time to socialise later.'

'They will be busy,' said Zee thoughtfully, 'laying carpets, plumbing in washing machines... too busy to even think about food, I expect. Why don't you take across some sandwiches, Mum? It would be very neighbourly.'

Her mother pushed her prematurely grey hair out of her eyes and wiped her hands on her gardening trousers. 'I'm far too hot and dirty, Zee. Besides, you're the sociable one in the family. You go.'

'Me?' she enquired as if the thought had never occurred to her. 'I suppose... if you really think I *ought* to... then I suppose I... *could*.'

'Go on – force yourself!'

'What about me?' demanded Gemma. 'I'm starving too, you know.'

'And I will be,' said Josh, 'soon as I stop feeling sick.'

'Okay, okay, I give in,' said Zee. 'Sarnies all round, then. Peanut butter or jam?'

The new people weren't answering. The third time Zee rang the doorbell, she kept the flat of her hand hard against it. A plate of sandwiches, perched waitress fashion on the finger tips of her other hand, wobbled precariously.

'Blrr-kk!'

The bell made a sound like an angry bluebottle, but again, nobody answered.

3

'Miguel Molotov,' murmured Zee, reading the name-plate again. 'Molotov, Molotov, Molotov.'

It rattled around her teeth like a dark exotic chocolate. The rest of the neighbours had boring names – Watson, Chambers, Young. Boring names for boring people. O'Keefe was as interesting as names got in Hazel Grove, and that one stuck out for all the wrong reasons. So there was no way, no way at all, that Zee was going back home until she'd found out what a Molotov looked like.

Just then a strange clamour started up inside. Roaring and grunting and banging mingled with a high-pitched tinkling sound. The door swung wide and Zee half expected some rabid beast to bolt past. Instead, the girl she had glimpsed earlier stared down the steps at her.

'What's that noise?' blurted Zee before she could stop herself.

'You might well ask,' came the reply. 'Believe it or not, it's a piano.'

'I didn't know they made sounds like that.'

'They're not supposed to – it's being tuned.'

Her voice was a bit posh, but her jeans, like Zee's, were torn at the knees and customised with felt tips. Zee glanced back at the nameplate. 'Tuned by Mi-gw-ell Mol-o-tov?'

'Good try,' said the girl cheerfully. 'It's pronounced Me-gel Molo-toff.'

'Right. Is he your dad then?'

Her face clouded as if a whole nest of hornets was stinging her on the inside. 'He's my Step,' she muttered.

'Er – Mum sent me over with these sandwiches.'

4

'That's awfully kind.' The girl hesitated. 'Look, if you could just try to ignore the racket...would you like to come in?'

Zee didn't need to be asked twice. She followed her into a long room with tall arched windows that reminded her of the assembly hall at school.

A team of removal men swarmed like Santa's elves around rolled-up carpets, and furniture in various stages of unpacking. Directing the operation was a small woman with curly hair and overalls. She seemed to know exactly where she wanted everything and she darted about deftly, clearing gangways and giving instructions. Oblivious to it all, in the middle of the room, Miguel banged away at a grand piano, shouting at it as if he expected an answer. His stepdaughter stood scowling at him but the woman, seeing Zee and the plate of sandwiches, swiftly crossed the room, covered his powerful hands with her own pale ones and dragged them off the piano keys.

'Calm down, Miguel, you're frightening the neighbours. You are a neighbour, aren't you?' she asked, smiling.

'Yes, I'm Zee Proctor from Number 5. Zee is for Zara.'

'I'm Tasha,' said the girl, 'this is my mum, Magda, and he's Miguel.'

Miguel gave an odd little half bow. He had frowns running down his forehead to each eyebrow which made him look incredibly scary.

'Would you like a sandwich, Miguel?' asked Zee bravely.

'You knows what they are?'

She swallowed a nervous giggle. Miguel's accent was fabulous. He tripped over his Rs and stretched his vowels like bubble gum. 'Of course – they're peanut butter.'

'Ah! In Bosnia this is a favourite.' He stuffed a big squelchy one into his mouth and a grin sent his frowns lurching sideways.

'Is that where you're from – Bosnia? I've never met anyone from that far away.'

He nodded. 'I am a long way from my home.'

'So it's wonderful to find the Irish as hospitable as everyone promised,' said Magda, helping herself.

Zee, looking properly at the sandwiches for the first time, felt herself blush. The filling was squelching out of the sides and her fingerprints were clearly visible in the peanut butter.

'Perhaps the removal men are hungry too, 'suggested Magda and at once they crowded around. It felt a bit like feeding pigeons; one minute Zee's hands were full of bread, the next there wasn't a crumb left.

'Why don't you take Zee through to the kitchen for a drink, Tasha?' suggested her mum. 'It's less chaotic in there.'

Their kitchen, thought Zee a moment later, was downright orderly compared to hers, even if they had barely moved in. She had never seen such a big fridge before. As big as a wardrobe it was with not one door but two. Eggs, pâtés and purées nestled beside rolls of salami and pastrami. There were a dozen foil-wrapped cheeses with impossible foreign names. Jars of dark pickle gleamed like medical exhibits and wraith-like herbs in bottles of golden oil glistened under the bright white light.

'Is it Bosnian?' whispered Zee.

'I don't think they've got food in Bosnia,' said Tasha loftily. 'All I know is I can't find a decent can of Coke! Would you mind sparkling grape juice instead?'

Zee shook her head. They just had apple juice at home, meal-times only mind, and diluted with lemonade to make it go further. She drank two long glasses of juice and ate continental bread sticks filled with chocolate. At least Tasha didn't complain about those.

'Will you be coming to school here?' Zee asked.

'Not likely! Mum says Belfast's still a war zone. Beats me why they agreed to come here at all. Especially *him*. Talk about out of the frying pan into the fire.' She laughed as if this was a private joke.

'There's been peace here for years now,' said Zee indignantly. 'Well, a sort of peace.'

'There's still trouble though – I've seen it on the news. Beatings and sometimes shootings too.'

Zee couldn't deny it. 'So you'll be going back to England for school?'

'In September. I board at a place called Redbales. Have you heard of it?'

Redbales – one of the most exclusive girls' boarding schools in England. Of course she had heard of it.

'My dad pays the fees – my *real* dad that is. He lives in London.'

'Do you see him much?'

'He's a businessman, dead busy.' She shrugged carelessly but Zee noticed that she also changed the subject. 'Have you been in this house before?'

'Only in the garden. When we were kids my big brother, Gary, and I used to ring the doorbell and run away. It's bigger than the other houses round here – we used to dare each other.'

Tasha wriggled in delight. 'Last open day at school we set off dozens of car alarms – we had parents and chauffeurs dashing about everywhere – it was wonderful!'

They laughed together. Wasn't it amazing how just one confidence could reveal a soul-mate? 'Where on earth did your mum meet Miguel?'

'At the refugee council, in London, where she worked. They've moved here to set up a programme for asylum seekers being settled in Northern Ireland. But that's bor-ing! What about you, Zee – got a boyfriend?'

'No.'

'Got your eye on one?'

'Maybe.'

Tasha beamed. 'So when do I get to meet him?'

'You don't. I don't either. I reckon guys are overrated – all pimples and wandering hand trouble. Anyway I'm outa here in three years' time – as soon as I get my A-levels. I'm going to travel to London, Paris, Prague. I'm not getting bogged down *here* with any guy.'

Tasha's almond shaped eyes widened in disbelief. You're going to live like a nun for three years?'

'Not exactly a nun...'

Her new friend grinned wickedly. 'No harm looking then, is there?'

Zee laughed loudly. After two weeks of unutterable boredom the summer holidays were looking up. She would get to know this family, especially Tasha who could be friendly and sophisticated, both at the same time. Just how did she *do* that? Perhaps it was something they taught at English public schools? Or perhaps it came from having such an exciting family. A rich daddy, a successful working mum and a musical Bosnian for a stepdad. Zee felt as if a passport to a whole new world had been thrust into her hands.

'We'll make the most of this summer,' she vowed. 'We'll have a *really* good time.'

'Deal!'

Miguel came in for a glass of water just then. 'You two could be twins, yes? Long blonde hair and the same size, I think.'

'Plump, you mean?' snorted Tasha. 'Thanks.'

Zee cringed and felt obliged to break the silence which followed. This was a bad habit of hers which usually only made things worse but somehow she couldn't stop herself. Zee hated silences.

'I don't want to be this size, I hope my puppy fat disappears soon,' she babbled. 'Dragging these thighs around is exhausting. As for my bum, it should have one of those signs you see on lorries saying, *Caution. Wide Load.*'

Tasha doubled up in peeling, over-the-top laughter.

Miguel, Zee realised, had not quite followed her rapid Irish accent.

'So, my dear,'he said. 'What does your parents work at?'

'There's only Mum,' said Zee. It was as easy as that, just three little words. Neither Tasha nor Miguel raised an eyebrow between them.

'What does your mum do?' asked Tasha.

'Nothing – well – lots!' Zee added guiltily. 'But she doesn't get paid for it, she doesn't go out to work. There are four of us kids, you see.'

'Four?' Surprise, or perhaps envy, skated across Tasha's face. 'Brothers and sisters *and* a mum who stays at home – you're *so* lucky.'

Zee stared at her. After all Tasha was the one with the expensive education, two dads and a fridge like Aladdin's cave.

'Let's do something tomorrow,' said Tasha as Zee was leaving.

'Tomorrow might be difficult. Mum wants me to go to a flaming peace demo.'

'Tomorrow evening then?'

'It's the eleventh night.'

'What?'

'The night before the Twelfth.'

'I can count up to twelve,' said Tasha with false solemnity. 'Whatever are you talking about?'

'The Twelfth of July. The anniversary of the Battle of the Boyne? When the Protestants thrashed the Catholics.'

'I must have missed that,' said Tasha. 'Was it on the telly?'

Zee's jaw sagged. How could anyone not know about the Battle of the Boyne? 'Doesn't 1690 ring any bells? King Billy and his Orangemen?'

'1690 ... gosh ... and this is 2004.' Tasha did a quick calculation. 'That battle was ... three hundred and ... er ... fourteen years ago.'

'So? It's what Ulster's all about! Doesn't your school do history?'

'Lord, not Irish history.'

'Now listen,' said Zee earnestly, 'on the twelfth of July there are marches all over Northern Ireland to celebrate the Battle of the Boyne. The night before – the eleventh night – the Orangemen kick it off with huge bonfires. It's surprising the whole of Belfast doesn't go up in smoke. There's singing and dancing and—'

'It sounds brilliant!' Tasha gripped her arm so hard it hurt. 'We *must* go.'

'Well – I'm not sure. Mum's not keen on that sort of thing – there can be trouble. I don't know if she'll let me go.'

'What about your brother, Gary? Will he be going?'

'Try keeping him away.'

'Then what's the problem? We can all go together, can't we?'

Zee bit awkwardly at her lip. 'Gary's not exactly ... reliable. He's a bit – um – a bit of a loner.'

Tasha's eyes rolled theatrically. 'Is he now ... that sounds like a challenge.'

'I'll try and talk Mum round,' Zee promised. 'Come over about seven-thirty – we'll do something.'

'It's got to be the bonfires!'

Zee ran down the steps, then she paused and turned back. 'Seriously, Tasha, forget Gary.'

'Whatever for?'

'Because he's not just a loner.' Zee took a deep breath. 'Gary's dangerous.'

2

When Tasha woke up, the first thing she saw was white plaster angels carved into the cornice high above her bed, and the first sounds she heard were Mozart's *Eine Kleine Nachtmusik* tinkling gently up through the hall.

Tasha scowled. Her mother had gone off to work in the city today, leaving her alone with Miguel. 10.07 said the digital read-out on her clock radio; it would be hours before her mother came back home again.

Tasha turned her TV and CD player up high enough to drown out the piano. Through the window she saw a blue and white electricity van pull up outside. She went to the bannister and yelled at Miguel to let the man in. By the time she went downstairs the meter man had gone, and Miguel was in the kitchen brewing coffee as thick as grit.

'You wants some?' he asked.

'No thanks,' she said, 'coffee's addictive.'

'Ah, for sure. You wants breakfast? I make it for you no problem.'

'That's okay, I'll just heat up some croissants.'

'Careful, I thinks croissants are addictive too.'

Tasha would have laughed if her mum had said that, but instead she just said, 'Yeah.'

Miguel cleared his throat. 'You wants to come to the shop later? I has to put an ad up for music pupils.'

13

'You're going to teach them here?' she asked him. She imagined the house overrun with screeching violinists and six-year-olds playing chopsticks interminably.

Miguel grunted. 'In Sarajevo I was Head of Music at the biggest high school in the city. In Belfast I suppose I has to start somewhere.'

'Suppose.'

'So, you comes for a walk?'

'Er...no, I've got to sort out stuff upstairs.'

'Okay, no problem.' He took his coffee back to the living room and a moment later he was at the piano again, bashing away hard this time.

The meter man turned out to be the first in a string of visitors. A plumber arrived to connect up the washing machine, then an electrician to mend the shower and another man to connect the telephone. Tasha found herself glad of the company; it made being with Miguel easier. At lunch-time she made herself a salad roll and ate it in her bedroom watching TV. When she went back downstairs she saw that Miguel had made himself something to eat too and he had washed up her mess as well as his own.

She explored the new house thoroughly, then went out into the garden. Grassy banks rolled down to an overgrown lawn edged with empty flowerbeds. When she took a stroll up Hazel Grove she realised that her house was bigger than the others, but somehow she liked Zee's house better. Number 5 was a pebble-dashed cottage, snuggled up in ivy, with bulging bay windows. The garden was full of pansies, nasturtiums and sweet

14

peas. It looked as colourful as a sweet shop, and beneath a tree, a little fountain gurgled. Someone had built a dinosaur-land around it, and in another shady corner hung a tree-swing. The place looked lived in and homely and Tasha felt a pang of envy.

Hazel Grove itself was just one single row of detached houses built on a hill. Each house was separated by a privet hedge and set well back from the red stone pavement in front. Opposite them, on the other side of the road, sprawled a wood with dirt tracks winding between trees and shrubs. A light breeze rustled the hazel leaves which twinkled like tiny flags in the sun. The only noise came from two little boys playing cars beneath a tree. Belfast seemed so peaceful.

It was five-thirty when Magda came back, the car boot filled with shopping.

'I could have done the shopping,' Tasha told her. 'You could have picked me up at Tesco's after work.'

'Great idea,' said her mum. 'Now I know where Tesco's is we can do that in future.'

'It's been dead boring here.'

Magda exchanged glances with Miguel who had staggered in the back door laden with shopping bags.

'I think you needs a glass of wine,' he announced.

'You're right, that's exactly what I need.'

'You puts up your feet. Tasha and I will puts these things away.'

. Tasha winced. She would have put the shopping away without Miguel suggesting it, and she used to be the one who sometimes poured her mum a glass of wine after

15

work. She pushed the groceries into the cupboards silently while Magda chattered about her new office, computer problems and colleagues she had made friends with already. When the groceries were packed tidily away, Miguel gulped a glass of wine and left the kitchen.

'What do you think of the house?' asked her mum.

'Great,' she admitted. 'Much nicer than that poky flat in Ealing.'

'Prices are lower here. The flat was all we could afford in London.'

'I like my room,' said Tasha. 'The telly, having my own space – it's good.'

'We thought you'd appreciate it.'

Tasha murmured, 'I suppose it keeps me out from under your feet too?'

'Hey! We want you under our feet – the more the better.'

'I should have thought you'd want time on your own.' Tasha sighed. 'I don't know why you didn't let me go on holiday with the Montgomery-Smiths. It would have been easier all round.'

Her mum got up and gave her a big hug. 'We want you with us, darling. We all need to spend time together, and you and Miguel need to get to know each other.'

'Yeah.'

Her mum chuckled and kissed the top of her head. 'Don't worry, it's early days – only six months since we married – and you've been at school most of that time.'

Thank God, thought Tasha, but she didn't say a word.

'So. Did you and Miguel do anything nice today?'

'I was busy unpacking,' she mumbled.

'Of course.' Her mother took a deep glug of wine. 'Well, we can do something together tonight. We've all been invited to dinner by one of my new colleagues. Isn't that kind?'

Tasha was horrified. It was bad enough skirting around Miguel at home all day; she could not possibly play Happy Families in public. 'I've got something on,' she cried.

'Oh?'

'With Zee. I'm spending the evening with her.'

'I haven't met her mother yet.'

'You've met Zee though. You liked her, didn't you?'

'Very much.' Magda was looking at her carefully. 'Oh, I suppose it will be all right. You'd better take the spare key, Tasha, I'm not sure how late we'll be.'

'Don't worry. I'm a big girl now, I can take care of myself.'

'You're fifteen,' said her mum. 'Make sure you're back by midnight. Now, I'm going for a bath – I've been fantasising about one all the way round Tesco's.'

Tasha listened to her exchange a few words with Miguel before thudding softly upstairs. She eyed up the wine bottle and, realising her mum would assume Miguel had finished it, and vice versa, she poured the remains into a mug and knocked it back. She spluttered as it kicked the back of her throat, but as the alcohol worked through her system, it eased her irritation and she relaxed.

Let Miguel and her mother get on with their lives. The

sooner they realised she had her own life, the better. Tasha turned her thoughts to the evening and felt a warm glow of anticipation. She had escaped Redbales for eight whole weeks. She already had a friend in this city and, what was more, that friend had an older brother.

3

Victims of violence proclaimed the banner on the city hall and beneath it, thousands of people had gathered for the peace demo. Heads bent, they listened to a Minister reading a verse, his voice floating down from the podium high above.

Yea, though I walk through the valley of the shadow of death I will fear no evil...

Zee groaned softly. Praying for peace seemed pretty ineffective to her, but her mum and all these people were heavily into it, eyes closed, as if the words were some magical incantation. It seemed forever before the Minister finished, then the tiniest children were marshalled into rows of four and began moving forward. Some of them were really tiny, helped towards the front by relatives and friends. Then it was the turn of the pre-school children. Next, the six-year-olds.

The twins took off as if it was sports day, practically racing across the grass to the long trestle table draped in red and tiered with white candles. Adults handed them tapers glowing at one end. Immediately, all the six-year-olds fell quiet, amazed at being allowed to handle fire and eager to do their bit properly. Josh and Gemma pressed their tapers solemnly against the wicks of two thick church candles. Zee held her breath until their wicks caught and the two tiny flames flickered. Her eyes burned unexpectedly and she had to blink.

'Next, children of seven,' called the voice and the twins came speeding back.

'That was cool!' cried Josh.

'Did we do it right, Mum?'

'Perfectly, Gemma.'

Zee heard a tremor in her mother's voice. She glanced nervously at her but she seemed to be holding things together pretty well.

'It'll be your turn soon, Zee,' said Josh, nudging her.

'I'm not doing it,' she muttered.

'You have to!' said Gemma.

'No, I don't.'

Sue bent down to them. 'Zee doesn't have to light a candle if she doesn't want to.'

'But it's for Daddy,' protested Josh. He turned and kicked a big divot out of the grass.

Zee glared at him. 'Don't you dare throw a temper on me, Josh Proctor. I'm not making a show of myself for anyone, right?'

Especially not for someone who's dead and can't even see, she thought. When they called her age group, she didn't move. She couldn't have moved, even if she had wanted to. The soles of her shoes felt super-glued to the ground. A moment later the woman next to her started crying. Soon, her mum and this total stranger were hugging each other and swopping horror stories. Zee wished that she was somewhere else – anywhere else. These peace demos always brought back bad

20

memories and upset folk. She couldn't see the point herself, they only made things worse.

When they called the adults forward, Zee held a twin firmly in each hand while Sue lit a candle. Her mother's head bent in prayer and it stayed bent for ages. Watching her, Zee felt a rock lodge in her own throat.

'Let's go now,' she said impatiently as soon as her mum returned.

'Steady, love. Someone's going to make a speech first.'

'And then we're going to sing a song,' said Josh.

'Not a song, silly, a hymn.' Zee listened irritably to the man at the podium. Did he have to be quite so negative about the bonfires?

'... *when sectarian fires burn tonight in every town across the province, your candles of peace will burn also, tonight when sectarian songs are chanted once again, your prayers of peace will be heard too. You, the victims of violence, the very people who have suffered most, demand that the politicians continue to seek peace ...*'

On and on and on ... Suddenly everyone was turning to the person next to them and shaking hands. Her mum hugged the stranger who had been upset. Zee had no intention of hugging a stranger so she hugged the twins instead. All around them people were laughing and crying at the same time. Then a piano struck up 'Rock of Ages' and after that, at last, they were on their way. There was a bit of a jam at the exit and in the hold-up people started talking about the latest violence, two punishment beatings in North Belfast.

'They're only isolated incidents,' said someone, 'nothing to threaten the peace.'

'Let's hope it stays that way for the next twenty-four hours,' came another voice.

Zee groaned. The last thing she wanted her mum reminded of was the possibility of trouble tonight. She still hadn't got a straight answer from her. Could she go to the bonfires with Tasha, or couldn't she? By the time they reached the car park, she was no wiser.

'For heaven's sake, Mum, I did what *you* wanted. I came to the peace protest, didn't I?'

'And now you want to go to the bonfires? Isn't that a bit hypocritical, Zee?'

'They're *only* bonfires.'

'They're a celebration of Protestant over Catholic.'

'It's just a bit of fun. Gary will be there, you know.'

'I wish he'd come to the peace demo with us.'

'Fat chance.'

As her mum tried to join the dual carriageway, Zee sank down into her seat, hoping that nobody in the other cars would notice her. They were moving far too slowly, forcing every car in sight to overtake them.

'Tomorrow, Zee...'

'Yeah, what about it?'

Her mother peered in the rear-view mirror at the twins. They were engrossed with their Action Man figures. 'Tomorrow I'm going to ask Gary not to march,' she said quietly.

Zee stared at her. Had she gone mad? Gary always marched. It was his big day. He and nearly a hundred other members of his Loyal Orange Lodge marched right through Belfast to the Field at Finaghy where all the different lodges met up and held a rally. 'Not march... when did you decide this, Mum?'

She didn't answer. That didn't surprise Zee really. Sometimes it took her mum the whole day to make the simplest decision, like what they would eat for tea that night, or how much coal she should order. It was one of the things that drove Zee mad. How had she ever made a decision this big?

'You won't be able to stop Gary,' she warned.

'I will. I won't give him Daddy's sash.'

Zee's breath was snatched away. 'Gary'll go mad – he'll explode!'

'I wish I'd stopped him marching two years ago,' said her mum. 'When I first thought of it. But he was hurting so much then, I thought marching might help him somehow.'

'Instead of which,' muttered Zee, 'he took up with Des Gordon and the rest of the brain-dead.'

They had lost speed again and Zee glanced at her mother. She was just hanging onto the steering wheel, not really driving at all. Tears began dribbling down her face. 'Oh, Mum, you've done so well today.'

'I'm sorry...'

'Don't say sorry, I hate that. Look, there's a lay-by coming up. You'd better pull over.'

They slowed to a halt just as a bicycle overtook them. Zee wrapped her arms around her mother and pulled her

23

close. This was the worst bit. Far, far worse than any-thing else. Seeing her own mum totally destroyed, and knowing that she could do nothing to help. She could not change a thing.

'I know a song that'll cheer you up,' shouted Josh and he started on 'Rock of Ages' again. Gemma joined in. Sue blew her nose on the kitchen roll she kept in the glove compartment in case one of them was sick.

'You okay, Mum?' Zee practically had to shout to make herself heard.

'Rock of Ages, cleft for me...' they sang as if they were on a Sunday school outing. They were used to their mum bursting into tears like this. It happened all over the place: in the supermarket, at school sports day, even at a filling station once.

'No,' Sue sobbed. 'I'm not okay at all. Sometimes I think it's getting easier, I think I've cracked it...then it comes at me all over again, suddenly, like a wild animal, like a tiger...it feels like being ambushed.'

'Can't you just avoid it?' asked Zee, but her mother shook her head.

Zee closed her eyes miserably and sat back while 'Rock of Ages' rang out from a lay-by on the A631.

It was 10.00 pm and starting to get dark but hordes of people were tramping down the Newtownards Road. Whole families were there, toddlers perched on their fathers' shoulders and children running alongside their parents. Crowds of teenagers shouted and joked as they headed for the fire.

24

In daylight, thought Zee, they would look like football fans. Only the songs were different. The odd snippet from a Loyalist ballad spiced the air, fading into laughter. Tasha linked arms excitedly.

'It's totally magic, Zee, I knew it would be.'

'We're not even there yet – you wait!'

Zee could hardly believe their luck. Her mum had kept her on tenterhooks until the last moment, and when Tasha arrived wearing a leather mini-skirt, and plastered in make-up, Zee thought their chances were zilch. But no, miraculously she had been allowed to go, after all, on condition that they stuck together. Now, spotting various school friends, Zee introduced them enthusiastically to Tasha.

'Hi, Tracey, Melanie, Pip! This is Tasha.' She just couldn't help adding, 'Her mum works with refugees – and her stepdad *is* one – they've only just arrived.'

'Most people are trying to get outa this country – not into it!' They fell around laughing. Zee smiled encouragingly at Tasha who was obviously finding the rapid Belfast dialect a little hard to follow.

'Have you heard from Jane lately?' Tracey asked.

'Jane was my best friend,' Zee explained. 'Her family emigrated to New Zealand at the beginning of the year.'

'You've got another best friend now,' said Tasha, grinning.

'You betcha!'

Suddenly they were there. Hundreds of people had gathered round a piece of puddled wasteland. For the rest of the year they would hurry past it without looking twice but tonight it drew them like a circus.

In the middle, the bonfire was built as high as a house. For weeks anyone turfing out furniture had thrown it onto the bonfire instead of taking it to the city dump. Sofas, wardrobes and beds all protruded at crazy angles from a haphazard pyramid of planks and wooden pallets.

'Save the rainforests!' shouted someone.

'Enough wood there to feed a sawmill,' said another man.

'Jackie, is that not your new three-piece suite I'm seeing?'

Zee enjoyed the crack right enough, but Tasha was like a tiny kid, twisting and turning, wide-eyed, determined to miss nothing.

'Who builds the fire?' she asked.

'Everyone who lives round here,' said Zee. 'Every house contributes.'

'Every Prod that is,' put in a man standing behind them.

'Protestant,' translated Zee.

'Won't there be any Catholics here, then?'

'Not if they've any sense,' said the same man.

Tasha lowered her voice and nodded. 'Over there, Zee! Are those real slums? Those little red-brick houses?'

Zee followed Tasha's gaze to the rows of terraced houses radiating out from the wasteland. 'They're not that wee! Two up, two down, Victorian back-to-backs you know. Built for the shipyard workers.'

'But they're identical...and so crammed together – like biscuits in a packet.'

'Doesn't mean they're slums.'

'I'll take your word for it,' said Tasha but she didn't sound convinced. 'Look! The fire! Is that safe?'

'Of course not!'

Three men were circling the bonfire, throwing petrol round the bottom of it, and chasing off small boys who were yelling and whooping with excitement. The men lit rags and hurled them in among the wood which began to crackle. Flames fanned out around the bottom and climbed towards the middle. Soon the belly of the fire was white, heat forcing the crowd backwards with a gasp. Higher and higher the flames crept, reaching for the wood at the very top until the whole crazy pyramid was alight. Three feet above it all, scarlet cinders caught in the draught, danced and glittered against the black night sky.

'Hello, Zee,' came a deep voice.

'Hello!' Zee glanced self-consciously around the crowd then back at the grinning face above her. 'What are *you* doing here?'

'It's a free country,' he said. 'I thought it was you I heard laughing. Who's your friend?'

Zee introduced them as quietly as she could. Tasha looked confused.

'I thought you said,' she began in her clear English voice, 'that any name beginning with O is a Cathol—'

'Ssh!' hissed Zee and whispered in her ear. 'Of course Con O'Keefe's a Catholic name. Heaven only knows what he's doing here but keep quiet – and don't use his first name either. Even that's a giveaway.'

Tasha looked flustered. Zee, remembering the peace protest earlier that day, stood on her tiptoes and said politely to him, 'You're very welcome here, you know.'

'Dunno if I'd go as far as to say that...but it's good to see you, Zee.'

There was something in his voice that reached right inside her and squeezed her stomach. His eyes held hers just a moment too long to be casual. They had lived in the same street for five years but she had never stood this close to him before. He had the most amazing melt-you-in-a-minute, drop-dead-dreamy-deep, coffee-coloured eyes. Zee almost fell over backwards looking up at them and her voice disappeared altogether. Fortunately she didn't have to speak because Conor started chatting to Tasha. Then the crowd crushed forwards, pressing her against him so hard that she could smell his soap.

'You okay?' he asked.

Before she could answer they saw the cause of the crush. A line of thugs, some with shaved heads, were trawling the crowd like a net. '*You* won't be OK,' Zee said nervously. 'Better lose yourself – quick!'

But it was too late. Two lads marched straight up to them. One with golden curls and biro-blue eyes planted himself right in front of Conor, hands on hips.

'Well, well,' he called out loudly, 'look what we have here, lads. A Fenian!'

Anticipation shivered across the crowd. For a moment all that could be heard was the frenzied crackling of the fire. People began edging back, their faces reflecting wild, cavorting flames. Zee could taste the smoke, the danger, even her own fear. She must overcome it, she had to speak out. She couldn't just stand by and see Conor get beaten up.

'Leave him alone!' she squealed, and then, finding more authority, she said, 'D'you hear me, Gary? Just you leave Conor alone.'

4

'*Your* Gary?' asked Tasha, her voice incredulous. 'He's your brother?'

'Yes,' Zee admitted and she felt shrunk somehow.

Gary was standing close up to Conor, eyeballing him like a boxer.

'What are you doing here?' he demanded, but before Conor could answer, the other youth butted in.

'And you, Zee? What the hell are *you* doing with the likes of him?'

'Mind your own business, Des Gordon!'

Her voice sounded an awful lot braver than she felt, and she shuddered as Des's eyes roved up and down her body.

'I just came over to say hello to Zee,' Con told them, 'that's all.'

'You stay away from her,' snarled Des. 'Stick to your own kind.'

Tasha cleared her throat but if she was trying to catch their attention she failed completely.

Gary punched Conor's shoulder, none too lightly. 'You should be at home, pillock. This is *our* night.'

Conor kept his balance, and looked Gary straight in the eye. 'There's supposed to be peace, isn't there? I can go anywhere I want.'

'In your dreams!' Gary hissed. 'Peace? Too many scores to be settled for that.'

'Not between us, Gary. It's not long since you and me were kids playing football in the street.'

Des moved in, pushing his fist hard into Conor's chest, forcing him back a step. 'You two were never mates, Fenian boy.'

'Stop it!' yelled Zee.

But Des had bunched Conor's shirt in his fists 'C'mon, Gary! Let's teach him a lesson!'

Excitement rocked those nearest in the crowd. Some folk turned on their heels and hurried off but others waited expectantly. The rest of the gang had gathered round and they began shouting and egging them on. Zee saw a baseball bat being shoved into Gary's hand.

'No, Gary, don't!' she screamed.

'O'Keefe needs a good kicking,' thundered Des. 'C'mon, Gary!'

Then came a new voice. 'Back off, Des, leave thon lad alone.'

It was a girl's voice and she sounded a whole lot calmer than anyone else. 'Ye heard me! Leave him be.'

The girl detached herself from the crowd, walked over and put her arm through Gary's. 'Ye headbanger! Put thon bat down before someone gets hurt.'

Gary hesitated for just a moment, then he tossed the bat back to its owner.

Zee stared in astonishment at this miracle worker. Dressed in a fringed black skirt and a black leather jacket, she wore a dozen silver earrings through her ears and nose and eye-brow, and her hair was as tangled as a road map. She was a few years older than Gary and she

31

spoke with a broad backstreet accent.

'Des,' she was saying now, 'let him go.'

'I'm gonna make sure he doesn't come back, Ruby.'

'He won't,' Zee put in earnestly. 'He's going home right now, *aren't you*, Conor?' But to her annoyance, Conor just stood there staring at Gary. Zee grabbed his arm and tried to pull him away. 'You come too, Tasha!'

Tasha didn't move either. She was gazing at Gary as if hypnotised. Zee couldn't believe it. Couldn't either of them see the danger they were in?

'I mean it, Gary,' said Conor quietly. 'I'd like to be friends.'

Gary swung right round and spat. Saliva glistened on Conor's boot. There was another sharp intake of breath from the crowd and Zee pulled Conor's arm even harder.

'For God's sake, c'mon!' she said. 'Tasha, let's go.'

'I think I'll hang out here,' replied Tasha.

'What? You can't! You're new here . . . you'll get lost.'

At that moment, Gary seemed to notice Tasha for the first time and he lost all interest in Conor. 'I'll take care of you, Tasha,' he said.

'Cool,' said Tasha, smiling at him.

'But we're supposed to stick together,' Zee reminded her.

Tasha was not listening. Gary was smiling back at her. Beneath the golden curls his face lit up like a neon light and, for a moment, even Zee could see that her brother was good looking. She glanced at the girl, Ruby, who had intervened, but she didn't seem to mind a bit. Only Des was still glowering.

'You should watch the company you keep,' he growled at Zee. 'And Gary – you should make her. I would if she was my sister.'

In the end Zee felt she had no choice but to leave Tasha behind; she could hardly force her home. Stares followed her and Conor as they threaded their way through the crowd and people nudged each other, whispering. It felt so sinister that Zee's heart thumped in her ears and she gripped Conor's hand tightly.

It's a celebration of Protestant over Catholic, her mum had said earlier. What if some other hot-head took exception to Conor's religion? What if they never got home?

Suddenly they were out, expelled from the crowd which closed like a zip behind them. Zee sucked in deep cleansing breaths of night air. The space around her had never felt so good, the long tongue of tarmac road in front had never looked quite so inviting. She gazed up at the Milky Way, a vast pin cushion high above them.

'Look at all the stars,' she enthused, overcome with relief. 'Millions of them stretching over whole continents! God, I can't wait to get out of this country!'

'Can't you?' Conor sounded surprised.

'No. Even if the peace works, it'll make no real difference – not deep down.'

'How d'you work that out?'

'It won't stop people hating each other. It won't take the religion or the politics out of them.'

'It'd be pretty dull if it did,' he said. 'But we can learn to live with each other.'

'I didn't see much sign of it just now. And *you* – why did you wind Gary up about being friends? Are you crazy?'

'I had my reasons,' he said darkly.

'Aye – pride. Honestly, boys!'

'Boys? I'll have you know I'm nearly seventeen.' He slipped his arm around her waist. 'All grown up. Shall I show you?'

'No!' She was amazed and thrilled and embarrassed all at once, but she spun out of his reach and passed it off with a laugh. Fancy making a move on her just now. Some fellas had no sense of timing.

'Are you training for a marathon?' he asked a moment later and she realised that she had quickened her pace so much they were practically running along the pavement.

'Sorry, I'm just fed up. I can't wait to get outa here.'

'So you said.'

'Tasha's travelled, you know. She's been all over the place on holiday.'

'Has she? It doesn't show.'

'I can't believe she stayed behind like that. You do think she'll be okay, don't you?'

'At Gary's tender mercy?' He laughed teasingly. 'Of course she will, Zee.'

'Don't you like Tasha?'

'I like you better.'

He grinned down at her and Zee's stomach somersaulted. 'I'm not going to be around much longer, you know. I'm going to be a journalist,' she said. 'In Fleet Street.'

'I'm impressed.'

Was he really? 'What about you, Con? You must have sat your GCSEs last month.'

'I want to do medicine eventually – if I get the grades. I'm aiming to be a surgeon one day.'

'A surgeon?' Zee really was impressed. 'Plenty of demand for surgeons if you stay here.'

'I plan to. And what will you do after Fleet Street, Zee?'

'I suppose I'll get assignments – Bosnia, Africa, the Middle East – anywhere but Belfast.'

He burst out laughing. He hooted and howled and practically doubled up.

'What's so funny?' she demanded.

'You are. Do you really think those places will be any different to here?'

'Of course they will. Stop laughing at me!'

'After what you did back there? I wouldn't dare laugh.'

But he was in stitches. She could see that by the streetlights and she could hear it in his voice. It was just that she hardly dared look at him now. She had always thought her neighbour was good looking, and now they were actually talking she felt all hot and bothered and confused. Thank heavens they were almost home. The lights were still on in her house and in Conor's house too, just a few doors up.

'I'm glad we bumped into each other tonight,' he said when they reached her gate.

'Aye, almost lynched we were – great fun.'

'Seriously, thanks. You're the bravest girl I know. Lucky for me you were there tonight.'

Zee felt ridiculously pleased. She had to look away to hide the blush that rose from her neck. 'I'm sorry about Gary,' she said.

'Don't you worry about him – I won't.' Conor kicked at a loose stone. 'So... d'you fancy going out some time?'

Zee's heart just about stopped altogether. She was grateful for the darkness; at least he couldn't see her face properly. 'Um...'

'We could go for a walk,' he suggested, 'take a picnic – tomorrow, maybe?'

'What about Gary?'

'No, I think we'll leave Gary behind.'

She laughed loudly. Conor was right; why should she let Gary rule her life? Maybe, like Tasha, she should grab her chances. 'A picnic sounds great,' she said.

'Well, I thought I'd better ask you before you make that dash for Fleet Street.' His eyes were twinkling as brightly as the stars. 'G'night, Zee.'

And he kissed her, ever so lightly, on the tip of her nose.

Tasha had never felt quite as lonely as she did when Zee disappeared into the crowd. The Irish were wild, weren't they? Everybody said so. What if they suddenly turned against her? What if Gary disappeared? She would be lost, totally lost, in a strange city.

'All right?' Gary asked, putting his arm around her.

'Yes, thanks.'

Someone threw him a can. He bent back the ring pull and lager frothed up with a hiss. 'Have a drink,' he told her. 'Enjoy the fire. In a wee while we'll move on.'

Tasha would have liked to ask where to, but instead she knocked back the lager coolly.

'So where is it you're from?' asked Des, and though he was the last person in the world Tasha wanted to talk to, it seemed only polite to answer.

'London,' she replied.

'Ooh!' he teased and some of the others laughed. Tasha might have fled if the girl with the broad accent had not came to her rescue just then.

'Better a plum in her mouth than straw in her head like ye, Des.'

'Nice one, Ruby,' yelled someone.

There was laughter, even applause. After that people were friendly enough but Tasha was relieved when the boys started talking among themselves, and she had a few moments to relax.

Huge flames still lunged heavenwards from the bonfire and the faces all around her were burnished with firelight. Tiny kids waved Union Jack flags and when an accordion struck up, folk began to sing along and dance. The air filled with beer and laughter again.

'Ciggy?' asked Ruby, and Tasha didn't refuse. She had smoked at school once or twice. What the hell?

Ruby blew out impressive smoke rings, 'So, ye fancy our Gary, d'ye?'

'That's my business,' said Tasha tartly but Ruby just

laughed. Between that and the cigarette, Tasha felt a bit silly. 'Okay, so I do fancy him. Does it show?'

'Just a touch.'

'Glad I'm amusing you.'

'Aw – don't be so starchy! We gotta get our laughs somewhere. God knows there's enough misery around.'

Tasha struggled to understand Ruby's accent but she knew the older girl would have buckets of useful info on Gary. 'Has he got a girlfriend?' she asked.

'No way. Plenty have thrown themselves at him, mind – includin' me.'

'You?'

Ruby laughed again and her big hair fluffed out. 'Aye, we had a wee fling in the early days.'

She shrugged as if it meant nothing to her, as if she had a million other lads queuing up to take her out, with her raggy hennaed hair and her cheap jingling jewellery. Tasha was not even sure that she believed Ruby. How could someone like her be so cheery about being dumped?

'Has Gary got his eye on anyone else?' she persisted.

'Only you, darlin'. I haven't seen that look in Gary's eye for a while.'

Tasha flushed happily but Ruby edged closer.

'Just don't expect too much of him, know what I mean?'

'Er – no ... what *do* you mean?'

'When I went out wi' Gary, it was like havin' a relationship with someone wearin' armour.'

Tasha bit back a bitchy remark. So Gary hadn't wanted to get close to Ruby? Surprise.

'We look out for him so we do – all of us,' said Ruby.

'Don't gangs always look out for each other?' asked Tasha.

'We're not a gang – just a crowd who hang out together.'

'I'll tell Conor that.'

Ruby stared at her, really stared. 'Ye don't know what I'm talkin' about, do ye? I thought his sister would have said.'

'Said what?'

'What happened.'

Tasha swallowed hard. She felt like a little kid again, left out, sent off to the playroom while her parents argued. She felt about five years old. 'So what did happen?'

'Their da was shot dead a coupla years back. Two hooded gunmen came to the house, murdered him right there in the livin' room.' Her voice dropped and she looked a little distant. 'The like of that's not supposed to happen in a livin' room, is it?'

Tasha stared back at her, horrified. 'I'd no idea,' she said at last. 'Oh, God! Poor Gary...poor Zee.'

Ruby nodded, making her metal jewellery clang. 'Afterwards Gary turned kinda bitter...closed off like. So, I'm just warnin' ye, don't expect too much from him.'

Zee's words yesterday evening came echoing back to Tasha. *There's just Mum*...she had said, and Tasha had assumed that meant her parents were divorced. After all, her own parents were divorced. Half the world was divorced or re-married. The fire roared in her ears. Being dead, let alone shot dead, had never even entered her head.

After that Tasha couldn't help staring at Gary. Every time he threw her a nod or a wink she smiled back. She had known right away it wasn't just his blue eyes and golden curls that attracted her. There was something more, something on the inside. Zee had called Gary a loner but Zee was wrong. Gary was just like her – *lonely* – which was quite different. Well, she could help him, she could be there for him.

Every time someone passed round a can, Tasha took a swig. She smoked till she felt sick. Later when they moved away from the bonfire it seemed the most natural thing in the world to link arms with Ruby and the rest of them, and sway through the backstreets together.

The backstreets. They were dark and exciting, like something out of the Dickens novels she studied at school. She tried not to stare at the tiny red-bricked houses with net curtains in the windows. The streets were barely wide enough for two cars to pass by. Red, white and blue bunting was strung between the houses like Victorian washing lines. Everywhere red, white and blue. Even the kerbstones were freshly painted in the colours of the Union Jack. Each individual house was flying a flag, the Union Jack or the flag of Ulster – a red cross on a white background with a clenched fist in the middle.

At the end of some streets huge murals were painted onto gable walls. King Billy astride a white horse seemed to be the favourite, riding high in detailed paintings of ancient battle scenes. And slogans everywhere.

No Surrender.

1690.

No Pope here.

Tasha had seen it on news programmes, of course, but it hadn't looked like this. It had been safe then, something happening hundreds of miles away. But this was here, now, above her, around her, plastered on every surface, so real it practically leapt off the wall, every figure poised to kill, every slogan screaming. Sirens wailed throughout the night as fire engines raced to douse bonfires and policemen took charge of street drunks.

Tasha had never felt so excited or so anxious. She kept Gary constantly in sight, worried that if she got lost in this city, she might never get back home. When they stopped to buy chips – real chips in real newspaper – she knew she had never tasted anything so meltingly delicious. The salt made the inside of her cheeks tingle and the warm grease filled up her stomach in a way that Redbales' low-fat oven chips never did. If only Gary would pay her a little more attention this would be the best night of her entire life.

At last he did. They all linked arms, three rows of six people – but Gary sought her out specially. He linked arms with her in the middle of the first row and they marched hard, tramping home through the backstreets, singing at the very top of their voices. Tasha's spirits soared even higher. She was wonderfully, deliriously happy and the verse they were singing was easy to pick up.

It is old but it is beautiful, and its colours they are
  fine
It was worn in Derry, Aughrim, Enniskillen and
  the Boyne.
My father wore it as a youth in bygone days of
  yore
And on the Twelfth I love to wear the sash my
  father wore!

It was a great tune and they fairly belted it out, yelling the word sash in the final line. Everyone laughed except Gary. His face was stern.

'What's wrong?' she whispered.

'They all think it's a joke,' he said tersely, 'just a song and a night out but they're wrong. They should sing the Sash with pride.'

'Have you got a sash?' she asked because she didn't know what else to say.

'Of course. My father wore it when he was young and his father before him and his father before him. And *I'll* be wearing it tomorrow.'

'Cool.'

Gary grinned. 'You're all right, you know.'

He put his arm around her shoulder and they started singing again, this time at the top of their voices, clapping their hands and stamping their feet. Once or twice an upstairs window opened. Whatever the resident said was drowned out by a torrent of laughter and abuse. Tasha, glowing with excitement, shouted as loudly as any of them. She had never had so much fun.

Gradually, the crowd dwindled. Ruby said goodnight and disappeared into one of the backstreet houses. In the early hours, Tasha and Gary peeled off too.

'Looks like you're making your own way home, Des,' shouted Gary over his shoulder.

Tasha giggled. 'He doesn't look chuffed. Was he expecting to walk home with you?'

'Yeah, Des lives in our street too. Right next door to the token Taigs.'

'The O'Keefes.' Tasha was beginning to understand street politics.

They were too tired to talk much but she snuggled up against Gary, tucked in beneath his shoulder. She had never done that before, not with any boy, and it felt like the most romantic thing in the world.

Gary held onto her when they reached her gate. His hands ran up and down her back, over her buttocks, around the hem of her short tight skirt and over the tops of her thighs. Tasha kissed him wildly.

'You're so sexy,' he said breathlessly. 'God, you're gorgeous.'

His lips fell on hers and his tongue, fierce and slippery, forced her lips apart. She jolted with surprise as his tongue searched her mouth, backward and forward, in and out, sliding over her teeth and tongue. She didn't like it much but at least he wanted to kiss her. In the end it was Gary who pulled away.

'I'll call you,' he said. 'Soon.'

43

5

Gary took a deep breath and sank beneath the water. Deaf, blind, weightless. He sometimes wondered if being dead would feel like this and he liked to practise. Once he had managed one minute, forty-two seconds. The water should really be cold, of course. Icy cold. His dad must be so icy cold by now. And the worms...

With a cry Gary broke the surface. He lay panting and the familiar bathroom irritated him. It was all so normal, so *nice*. Toys in lurid colours were scattered across the plastic shelf bridging the bath; Gemma's tea-set in sickly scarlet and yellow, Josh's blue and orange lifeboat. Its captain with his stupid grin plastered forever across his face.

In a temper, Gary lifted one leg clear of the water and kicked the shelf hard. The toys shot off, hit the window, ricocheted against the wall and fell to the floor. He lay still for a moment, listening. There was no sound. Why would there be, he thought bitterly. The rest of them were still fast asleep. Hadn't they all given up on the Twelfth except him?

Five minutes later, dressed in his dark suit, he slipped across the landing to the big chest and eased open the top drawer. Surprise speared through him; the precious case had gone. The slim leather case that held the family sash was nowhere to be seen.

He started searching methodically from left to right then he tried the next drawer down. By the time he got to the fourth drawer he knew he wasn't going to find it. His mother slipped out of her bedroom like a ghost.

'Where's the sash?' he demanded.

'It's not there, Gary.'

'So where is it?'

'It's safe, I promise you.'

'And Grandpa's war medals – what have you done with them?' he cried.

'They're safe too, don't worry.'

'*Where are they?*'

'Listen to me, Gary. I don't want you to wear them today.'

'Don't be daft, Mum, it's the Twelfth. I need the medals, sash, the lot!'

'Your father hadn't marched for twenty years, Gary, maybe it's time you stopped too.'

He looked at her properly now. She was fully dressed, wide-awake, her face washed out and grey. She looked as if she had hardly slept at all.

'*I march,*' he told her grimly, 'and I always will.'

Zee emerged, yawning, from her room and Gemma followed, fumbling with her dressing gown. Then Josh came out of the third bedroom and they stood there, the four of them, lined up on the landing as if they shared some big family secret. Gary felt his temper slipping again.

'Just gimme the box,' he said. 'It's time I was on my way.'

'We need to talk,' said his mum.

'Not now!'

'Yes, right now. I've been trying to speak to you for weeks, Gary, but you're forever diving off. Well, it won't wait any longer – so you'll listen now.'

He glanced pointedly at his watch. 'Five minutes then.'

'I mean it, son, I don't want you marching today.'

'Why the hell not?'

'Because it's time to move on.'

'Move on? What is this?' He heard himself shout but he didn't care. 'What are you talking about?'

'Northern Ireland has the chance of peace,' his mother said. 'You can go to a football match now, Gary, without hearing bombs and sirens. You can take a girl to the cinema and know the buses will still be running when the film's over. You can even go for a job anywhere you want in this city without being afraid some gunman's going to grab you on the way.'

'You sound like a politician,' he scoffed.

'The politicians are trying to put things back together! And you, Gary – you've got to get on with your life. Put things behind you, get a job, get some money – enjoy yourself.'

'I can't believe I'm hearing this,' he said angrily. 'Is that it? Sermon over?'

'It's what's the rest of us are doing,' said Zee in that infuriating, superior way of hers.

'Bully for you!' he snapped. 'I've wasted enough time. Give me the medals, Mum. Give me the sash.'

Their eyes locked and his mother shook her head. For once Gary wavered. Usually he did exactly what he wanted, took what he wanted, but he wasn't going to lash out at his own mother. Zee, he could have sworn, was smirking.

Suddenly it all made sense. 'This is *your* idea, Zee, isn't it? You put Mum up to this.'

'I did not!'

'I bet you did. After last night, I wouldn't put anything past you.'

'I never!'

'What happened last night?' asked their mother quickly.

'Nothing,' said Zee but she went blood red.

Gary wagged his finger at her, just managing to keep his temper. 'She was only hanging off the arm of a Fenian, Mum. That's all!'

'Liar!'

'I thought you went to the fire with Tasha.'

'I did, Mum. Conor just happened to be there.'

'That had better be true,' shouted Gary. ''Cos if I find out different...'

'You'll what?' sneered Zee. 'Get a life, Gary. Why do you *want* to hang around with those sad little pals of yours? Why d'you *want* to get dressed up today and march round like a clockwork bloody penguin?'

Something snapped inside him. He flew at her, gripped her shoulders, shook her hard. 'Have you forgotten our dad completely?'

'Stop it!' shouted their mother. The twins squealed and fled behind her.

But Zee wouldn't squeal, no matter how hard he

47

shook her. She just stared at him, contempt pouring from her eyes.

'Go on,' she goaded. 'Hit me! I bet hitting girls is just your style . . . big man that you are.'

'Hit you?' He gripped her even harder and had the satisfaction of seeing her flinch. 'If I ever find you with O'Keefe again, I'll kill the both of you and that's a promise, *Fenian lover*!' He shook her till her hair flew like a rag doll's. 'You're a Prod and you'd better remember it!'

'Gary – leave her be this minute!' Their mother was prising his fingers off her.

Gary flung Zee back against the wall, then he charged downstairs and out of the house. Empty-handed.

Zee slid down the wall, clutching the tops of her arms. In films it seemed melodramatic when people slid down walls but she understood why they did it now. The wall felt so solid, one firm contact when everything else was reeling.

'Zee . . . Zee . . . are you all right?' asked her mother anxiously.

'Yeah . . . yeah, I am.'

'Let me see.'

Gary's fingermarks stood out like bunting against her skin.

'Cold water for bruising,' said her mum mechanically but she didn't move and her hand shuddered up to her mouth. Zee's eyes filled with tears that didn't fall, like gutters blocked in a rainstorm. The twins stood staring at her, holding hands tightly.

'Josh, fetch me a sponge soaked in cold water, there's a love.'

Josh ran to the bathroom and came back with a sponge dripping all over the carpet. Gemma fetched a towel, then disappeared again and returned with one of her dolls.'

'You can cuddle my Barbie,' she offered. 'Or me.'

She leapt into Zee's lap, hugging her fiercely. The tears spilt out then and fell down Zee's face. Her mum went on sponging carefully.

'It's brandy people need when they have a shock,' said Josh. 'Do you remember after Daddy died? I never got any that time.'

'And you'll get none now! Away and put the kettle on – sweet tea does the trick just the same. I'll make us all a cuppa tea with lots of sugar. Then you two can go outside and play in the sun.'

Zee expected the Spanish inquisition from her mum, but after they had drunk the tea, she was sent back to bed to rest. She didn't think she would sleep but she did, and when she woke, the room was stifling. The sun shot like a laser through the window and dust particles danced in the beam between the two coombs of the ceiling. Outside Zee heard the little fountain piddling away. She wondered if Tasha had got safely home last night. What had happened between her and Gary?

She stared at the white flecks in the lilac wallpaper. She and her mum had put it up together, six months after Dad died. Zee had wanted to re-decorate the whole house but her mum hadn't the energy for decorating and, anyway, Gary wanted everything kept just the same. Except the living room of course.

They had to get decorators in to do the living room. She remembered the whirr of the steam cleaner and how Gary had stuck his fingers in his ears to block out the sound. They had put up pale green paper which Zee liked but Gary would not even go into the room for eight whole days.

'You look brighter,' said her mum when she went downstairs. 'More tea?'

'If you promise not to poison it with sugar again.'

'Sit down. How's your headache?'

'Still there. Gary's probably given me concussion.'

'Maybe I should call the doctor.'

'Or the police.' Zee didn't really mean it but she wanted to say it anyway.

Her mother poured the tea. 'I don't know what to do with him, Zee. Maybe counselling's what he needs but he won't hear of it.'

'What he needs,' said Zee angrily, 'is someone his own size to sort him out.'

'Someone like Conor?' she asked.

'What?'

'Zee, be careful. Don't you go making things worse.'

'Me? How could I do that?'

'By going out with Conor. By winding Gary up.'

Zee spluttered on the tea. 'So this is *my* fault, is it?'

'Of course not. But why *were* you with Conor last night? How did you expect Gary to react? You were supposed to be with Tasha.'

'I told you, we just bumped into Conor.' She did not see any point in telling her mum that Tasha had practically swooned into Gary's arms, then deserted her. 'Gary and Des started giving Conor a hard time, so they did. I just suggested he went home before there was a fight. We walked back together – that's all.'

'Honestly?'

'Yes!'

Her mother sighed. 'The lad must be a bit of an eejit, anyway, going to the bonfire – I've never heard the like. For a moment I thought you and he had something going. That's a relief, anyway.'

'You're a right hypocrite!' Zee banged down her mug, spilling tea on the table. 'Some peacemaker *you* are. You want Catholics and Protestants to live together – aye – as long as we don't actually speak to each other!'

'That's not true. Hazel Grove's a mixed area and I get on with *all* my neighbours. I'm just saying we need to make allowances for Gary.'

'Allowances? It was *your* idea to stop him marching, Mum.'

'I know.'

'Well he took it out on me!'

'I'm sorry, Zee.'

'He'll go to the Field, you know, even if he doesn't march.'

'We have to be patient. Don't push him, Zee.'

'Patient? He gets away with knocking me about and *I* get the row?' Zee jumped up, furious. ' I'm outa here!'

'Come back! What about your hcadachc?'

'You're only making it worse!'

She strode straight past the twins, across the road into the wood and down to the river. Her head thumped. She was supposed to be meeting Conor for a picnic in less than an hour. Lying back against the bank, she wished she could think straight. She didn't know what to do.

Eventually she scrambled up the bank again and walked through the wood, emerging opposite the O'Keefes'. In the next house, nosy Mrs Gordon shrank back behind her nets. Zee waved at her enthusiastically as she marched up to Conor's front door.

'Hi,' he greeted her. 'You're early.'

'Can I come in?'

'Of course. We'd better go into the front room. It's like a zoo through the back.'

Zee could hear it. There were eight O'Keefe boys and Conor was the oldest. No wonder his mother always looked worn out. The noise rose, they all seemed to be shouting at once. The smallest one, Diarmaid, burst into the hall crying.

'I want my mum!'

'You know she's out,' Conor told him. 'What's wrong?'

'Sean hit me so he did! Just 'cos I wouldn't give him my car.'

Conor scowled at Diarmaid in exasperation and Zee could imagine how embarrassed she would feel in the same circumstances. 'It's okay,' she told him, grinning. 'You'd better go and sort them out.'

'Go through,' he told her, 'I'll be back as soon as I've read the riot act.'

Zee had only been in one other Catholic house before. That belonged to the MacGuinesses who were the only other Catholics in the street. They had a sauna and a wide-screen television and Mrs Gordon said they made their money smuggling guns.

Waiting in the front room, she scrutinised the glass ornaments on top of the sideboard. There were only jugs and vases. She had expected to see shrines of the Sacred Heart, and great crucifixes on the walls with Jesus hanging off them, dripping blood. She had heard, too, that Catholic houses always smelt of saturated fat because they ate unhealthy diets, but this room was bright and airy and the smell of honeysuckle wafted in through the window.

'Looking for something?' asked Conor.

Zee jumped. 'I was just—'

'Curious...I know...like me last night.' He smiled and her stomach went jittery all over again. 'Cuppa?'

'No fear,' she said. 'I've had enough tea today.'

'Is there a problem?' He was studying her and in daylight his eyes were the colour of caramel.

'Conor, I-I've changed my mind about going out today. I'm sorry.'

She saw a big shutter come slamming down behind his eyes. He was upset. 'It doesn't matter, Zee – no sweat,' he said.

'You don't understand.'

'Sure I do – cold light of day and all that.'

'No!' She couldn't let him think that, it wasn't fair. 'It's not you, Con, really it isn't.'

'So what is it then?'

She frowned, wishing she had worked out what to say.

He stared at her. 'Is it Gary? It *is* him, isn't it?'

'Mum wouldn't give him Dad's sash this morning. She told him to stop marching.'

Conor whistled, a low admiring whistle. 'That was brave.'

'Aye, but he blamed me,' she blurted.

'Did Gary hurt you?'

'No, but he told Mum you were there last night. It came out that you and I walked home together. The thing is...it's not only Gary. Mum doesn't want us going out either.'

'I see.'

'No, you don't! She's not prejudiced. She's always dragging us off to peace protests. And she has nothing against you. She's just scared.'

'Scared of Gary?' he asked.

'She thinks he'd go mad.'

Conor's eyes narrowed. 'Are you sure he didn't hurt you?'

She nodded but she couldn't meet his eyes.

He took her gently by the arms, but it was just where Gary had bruised her and she breathed in sharply.

'What the—?' He pushed up the sleeves of her tee-shirt. 'The bastard! How *dare* he?'

'So now you see! Conor...*us*...it's just not worth it.'

His mouth twisted in silent protest, then he put his arms very carefully around her and held her close. They felt so wonderful there, so right.

'If he ever hurts you again,' said Conor, 'if anyone does, I'm here for you, understand?'

Zee glowed, she could barely speak; no boy had ever made her feel this special. 'Thanks, Con.'

'I'll always be here for you, Zee.'

Through the window she saw his mother coming in the little wicket gate. Conor saw her too and he pulled Zee out of sight behind the curtain.

'Would she go mad too?' whispered Zee, and in spite of everything they laughed. Parents, who'd have them?

'She'd convince herself I'd get beaten up,' he admitted.

'She'd probably be right. Maybe it's for the best. Will you be okay?'

'Don't you worry about me. I'll sign on with a dating agency. I bet they'll set me up with some frosty ould librarian with a passion for archaeology.'

Zee didn't look at him again. She didn't want to see his big soft eyes and his warm smile. She was liking him far too much already.

6

It was Friday night but Zee had still not quite forgiven Tasha for deserting her. '*If* we go out tonight, do you *promise* to stay with me?' she demanded. 'Right to the bitter end?'

'Yes! Of course I will. I have said sorry.'

'Hmm... Anyway, there aren't any discos on.'

'We could go to the Co-op,' said Tasha. 'It's been a whole week since we went anywhere.'

'Not the Co-op,' groaned Zee. '*Please* not the Co-op.'

Her eyes watered as she applied the charcoal eye-liner that was part of Tasha's huge range of make-up. Apparently her father sent her an allowance every month. Zee could not help being just a tiny bit envious; it would have taken her six whole months to save up for this lot.

'You told me yourself,' Tasha continued, 'that the football pitch behind the Co-op is where the crowd hangs out.'

'It is, but don't you think it's a bit uncool to – er – chase guys?'

Tasha shrugged carelessly. 'I'm sure there's a very good reason why Gary hasn't been in touch with me.'

'Maybe.'

Zee had not shown Tasha her bruises, or even told her about the blow up with her brother. Something, some sense of family loyalty, stopped her. She even felt a little guilty now. Maybe she had wound Gary up a bit, like her mum said. Maybe *she* was the reason that he hadn't rung Tasha.

'I know why you're being such a bore,' said Tasha crossly. 'It's because of that Conor O'Keefe, isn't it?'

'Could be.'

'It was your decision not to see him again. I really don't understand what the problem is.'

'I just didn't think I'd feel this down about him.'

'Then all the more reason to get out and have fun.'

'You're probably right – but I can't think of anything less fun than spending Friday night with my dead end brother and Desperate Des.'

'But *I* want to. Oh, come on, Zee. What else is there to do?'

'Nothing,' she admitted.

Tasha rolled her made-up eyes lavishly. 'I shall explode if I have to sit around here for another evening.'

Zee could have stayed in Tasha's room for ever. On the TV a good-looking black guy was dancing, though they had turned down the volume to listen to CDs. Tasha had lit some beeswax candles and the flames were reflected in the floor length mirrors that covered one wall. There was a rug with a tiger's head on the floor, and she even had her own ironing board set up in one corner. It seemed so adult compared to Zee's room. She cringed at the thought of the shelves crammed with Gemma's cuddly toys, the big doll's house and the boxes packed with dog-eared children's books.

Suddenly Tasha whipped a bottle of Bacardi out of her own personal Ali Baba laundry basket and splashed it into both their Cokes.

'No!' squealed Zee, then she took an experimental sip. 'Actually, that's quite nice. Natasha Molotov, you are wicked!'

'Natasha Cooper, if you don't mind.' Tasha giggled at her. 'You look ridiculous, you know. Sit still and I'll do a repair job. Your eyes look like you've risen from the gra—'

Zee glanced up at her in surprise. Tasha had frozen. 'The grave,' Zee finished. 'So Gary's told you about our dad?'

'I'm so sorry – it...it must have been truly awful. Trust me to put my foot in my great big mouth. I really am sorry, Zee.'

'No sweat, I'm over it.'

'Are you?' Tasha was watching her in the mirror.

'Of course. It was more than two years ago, you know.'

'Why didn't you tell me?'

'Why should I?' She sounded harsh so she added, 'Talking won't bring him back, will it?'

Tasha gulped her drink and brushed mascara onto Zee's eyelashes in silence. Zee was thinking hard. If Gary had already told Tasha about their dad, perhaps it meant there really was something between them. Perhaps it was wrong of her to hold them back.

'I suppose,' she said at last, 'we could go to the Co-op just this once. But it'll be *really* boring. They'll all be getting drunk on cheap cider.'

58

Tasha beamed at her. 'I think I can find something more exciting than that,' she said.

Something more exciting turned out to be a bottle of wine which she filched from the living room sideboard.

'You can't do that,' whispered Zee in horror. 'That's stealing!'

'Not really, not as if it's from a shop or something.'

'But it's not yours!'

'Cool it, Zee. It really doesn't matter.'

'But... won't they miss it?'

Magda and Miguel came into the room at just that moment. Tasha slipped the bottle into her bag and spun round just in time. She didn't look at all cool now. She had turned bright red and Zee could feel her own cheeks burning too.

'What are you two up to?' asked Magda with a grin. Miguel was not laughing however. He was staring at Tasha, his heavy tanned face swallowed up in one huge frown. He said something to Magda in his own language and she answered him briefly.

'Miguel is wondering where you're off to,' said Magda, 'dressed like that?'

'Like what?' demanded Tasha rudely.

'Without your clothes on,' said Miguel, his top lip curling in distaste.

Zee spoke before Tasha could do any more damage. 'We're just going to meet up with my brother. We're not going to a party or anything.' Privately, she had already thought that Tasha looked a bit tarty in a short suede skirt and a skimpy top that showed off her pierced belly button.

'In Bosnia we have a word for girls who dress like this.'

'So do we,' snapped Tasha. 'Fashionable!'

'Pah!'

'Zee is a bit more covered up,' said Magda gently.

Zee, who was wearing jeans, brushed the comment aside airily. 'Oh, I just couldn't be bothered tonight...'

'We'll see you later,' announced Tasha and she tried to march out of the room. Miguel lifted her red silk jacket off the couch and held it out to her, blocking her way. Tasha scowled at him, scandalised. 'It doesn't even match!' she told him. '*Mum*?'

There was a moment's thorny silence and Zee braced herself; no way was she going to break this one.

'Take it,' said Magda.

Tasha turned her scowl on her mother, as if she had been betrayed, then she snatched the jacket from Miguel and walked haughtily out. Zee hurried after her, whispering, 'Corkscrew!' into her ear.

Complaining bitterly, Tasha got stuck into the wine right away and by the time they had left the red stone pavements of Hazel Grove behind, she was ranting.

'Just who does he think he is? He's not my father.'

'It's just different cultures, Tasha, different outlooks.'

'Yeah, well he can keep his! I wish he'd go back to bloody Bosnia.'

'He can't,' giggled Zee. 'That's the whole point of being a refugee. They can't go back.'

'So why did *my* mum have to take pity on him? We were all right before he came along, you know. Following her around all day like a big bloody dog! He's not got any money, you know. He's living off us!'

'They're married, Tasha, they're in love! I think it's dead romantic. You'll soon get used to him.'

'Pah!'

'See? You're picking up the lingo already.'

Tasha laughed in spite of herself. She started playing hopscotch on the paving stones. She leapt onto all the cracks, stretching her legs wide to reach the edge of the paving stones, then bringing her knees close together to balance on the crack in the middle.

'You're doing it all wrong,' Zee called. 'You're supposed to land on the paving slabs and avoid the cracks.'

'Cracks are more fun,' announced Tasha. 'Live dangerously – that's what I say!'

'Just how much have you drunk?'

Tasha didn't answer. Zee seemed to have some catching up to do. She didn't approve of Tasha nicking the bottle of wine, but she didn't want to be the only person stone cold sober this evening. She raised Tasha's shoulder bag to her lips then hopscotched after her new friend. For the first time in a week she felt happy.

They jumped over the Co-op fence onto the edge of the football pitch and collapsed in a giggly heap on the other side.

'Oh no, there's Gary,' whispered Tasha although he was a hundred yards off. 'And I've got burps!'

'He's got his arm around someone,' said Zee, 'the poor girl.'

'It's that Ruby.'

61

Zee giggled again. 'Are you growling, Tasha?'

'I shall tear her head off.'

'I wouldn't bother, she looks like she could knock you flat.'

Tasha need not have worried about her burps because Gary didn't seem to notice her at all for the first half hour. They hung about pretending to watch six boys kicking a ball between goalposts at one end of the pitch. The rest of the crowd, perhaps a dozen in all, stood smoking and passing round cans of lager. It was every bit as brain-numbingly dull as Zee remembered from her first brief visit there a year ago. Then, out of the corner of her eye, she saw Des nudge Gary.

'They're coming over, Tasha, look.'

But Tasha had whirled round so they couldn't see her face and she was hopping about again just like she had that night at the bonfire.

'Gary looks embarrassed,' hissed Zee. 'So he should – the rat – he should have phoned you. Give him a hard time, Tash!'

'Hi,' said Gary, his eyes bright beneath his curls. 'Good to see you, Tasha.' He ignored Zee completely but Des treated her to a ghastly rubber lipped smile. Zee squirmed and tried to hide behind the bottle of wine.

'Hello, Gary,' replied Tasha, coolly.

'I'm glad you came,' he said.

'Are you?'

'Yeah.'

Why did nobody at the field ever speak in words of more than one syllable? Zee wondered impatiently.

'Haven't you got something else to say to Tasha?' she demanded. 'Something beginning with S?'

'Zee, don't,' begged Tasha, blushing.

'Yeah, keep out of it!' Gary scowled at her ferociously, but he added, 'I've been kept busy – it's the marching season.'

'Is that it?' Zee's tongue was loosened by the drink. 'That's your apology, is it?'

'Butt out,' said Gary. 'Something came up, that's all.'

Yeah, your fists, thought Zee but she said nothing. Tasha seemed satisfied anyway and Zee watched her arrange her face provocatively, lips pouting, eyes narrowed. She had never seen that done before, not outside a cinema anyway.

'If you promise to be a good boy,' said Tasha temptingly, 'I might give you some of my wine.'

For a short time they were the most popular people on the field. Then, with the wine finished and dusk beginning to thicken, couples started to migrate towards the long grass between the edge of the football pitch and the big Co-op building.

Zee and Tasha stood beside the Co-op wall discussing new films with some other girls. No one was interested in the films, really. It was just something to talk about, a cover for all the meaningful expressions and nudges that were flying around. Everyone had their eye on someone. Everyone, thought Zee, except her.

A group of boys, including Gary, stood nearby, their voices frequently rising in laughter or obscenities. Every few minutes, a boy would detach himself from that group and wander casually over to theirs.

– 'Stuart was wondering if Karen wanted to go with him.' –

There would be a long pause while Karen took advice from the girls.

– 'His brain's tiny.' –

– 'Aye, it's even smaller than his other bits.' –

– 'In that case Stuart should be in the Guinness Book of Records.' –

After shouts of laughter Karen would give her answer. 'Tell Stuart I'd rather go with his granda!'

Zee found it all a bit tedious but Tasha seemed to be enjoying herself. As the evening wore on, people paired off. In the end Tasha and Zee were the only girls left. Worse still, Gary and Des were the only boys.

'Let's go,' said Zee anxiously. 'I've had enough.'

'Not yet.'

'I feel a bit light-headed, Tasha.'

'Don't you dare bottle out – Gary's coming over.'

'So is Des! Oh no...do you *really* want me to stay, Tash?'

'Yes! Stick together – remember?'

'Okay, we'll meet round the other side of the Co-op at a quarter to twelve. No later, mind. If I'm not in by twelve I'll get grounded.'

Tasha glanced at her watch. 'But it's twenty past eleven already.'

'Good, I've got Frankenstein's monster, remember?'

Gary and Des had drifted within earshot. Undeterred, Des grinned at her.

'All right, Tasha?' asked Gary.

'Well, things could be better,' she said.

'Is that so, now? Fancy a wee walk?'

'That rather depends on Ruby,' said Tasha loudly. She sounded drunk.

'Ruby?' He looked puzzled. 'Ruby Mason? She's gone to a party.'

'So you're coming on to me now? Is that it?'

Gary laughed. 'Ruby's just a friend, Tash.'

'She wasn't always. She told me so herself.'

'Well, she is now.' Gary shifted his feet, shrugged, grinned, and generally managed to make himself look boyishly endearing.

Zee groaned. She had seen it all before with other friends. Gary hardly had a sophisticated patter but he always seemed to get the girl he wanted. Some of her friends used to come to the house just to see Gary.

'How could you think there was any competition?' he was saying now. 'Sure you're gorgeous.' Tasha turned pink and he held out his hand. 'C'mon.'

'You okay, Zee?' asked Tasha.

'Sure,' she said but her stomach felt as if someone had just pulled the plug out of it. She watched them pick their way over the tussocky grass in the darkness and heard Tasha laugh at some remark Gary made, then toss her head backwards, all elegant and sophisticated. Somehow it made Zee feel horribly inadequate.

Des was leering at her. However else she might try to think of it, he was definitely leering, mostly at her bottom.

'Looks like it's you and me,' he said cheerfully.

She tried to smile. If there was anything in the world worse than being left with Des, it was being left without him, entirely alone, silhouetted against the interior lights of the Co-op while everyone else snogged. She really did not want to stand there all alone for the next twenty minutes while couples entwined in the grass giggled about her.

She rapidly ran through her options. She could tell Des that she was going home then scuttle round the other side of the building to wait for Tasha. But Des would pass her on his way home. What would he think then? What would he say? Would he spread rumours about her? Say she was just a kid? A scared kid? And maybe, just maybe, she was ...

'We could go over there,' he said, nodding towards a bush.

'I don't think so.'

'Ah, c'mon!'

'No, I'm staying right here.'

'Have it your own way,' Des said and the next moment his arm shot round her like a chain. 'You know I've always liked you, Zee ...'

'I've got to go soon,' she gabbled, 'gotta be in by midnight.'

Des lifted her chin and fastened his mouth on hers. It felt like it was clamped on then his tongue wiggled through and wrapped itself round hers. She tried to pull away. She wanted to spit, to get rid of the horrible smoky taste of him and the wormy texture of his tongue, but she didn't dare.

He pushed her back slowly until she was pinned against the wall. She could see the moon reflected in a puddle between the distant goalposts. Des was pawing all over her and she wasn't sure how to stop him. Perhaps it was the alcohol but she felt detached, as if she was floating outside herself watching what was happening to her body, watching it happen to someone she hardly knew.

His hand groped across her jersey, then he dived underneath it. She wondered how close Tasha and Gary were. Close enough to hear her scream no doubt, but she knew she wouldn't scream. She couldn't. They would think she was such a baby.

Des had hands like shovels and he was digging under her bra now, scratching her skin with his dirty finger-nails, tugging impatiently at the tight fitting cotton. Eventually it gave and she heard a little moan of satisfaction as his hand squeezed her breast.

'That's sore!' she said.

She pulled his hand out but he gripped her own hand and pushed it between his legs. She felt a long hard lump and pulled away in fright.

'Stop it,' she hissed. 'That's enough!'

'It's all right.'

'It's not!' she said, furious.

How had she got herself into this situation? Why couldn't she extricate herself? Tasha would know what to say, what to do. Des was at her breasts again, and sucking her neck like a pig as he manoeuvred his body on top of hers.

He was as heavy as a pig too and he smelt of sweat and lager and cigarettes. Zee found that she could hardly move, could hardly even breathe. Somehow she managed to lift one arm and her watch said eleven-forty two. There was no sign of Tasha.

'Stop it!' she told him again and hammered on his back with her free fist. 'I've gotta go.' Des was fumbling with the metal button at the top of her jeans now, swearing under his breath. 'I said stop it, Des!'

'Shut up,' he grunted.

Panic shocked through her. His voice was hard and terse; she hardly recognised it. What was he doing? Surely she wasn't going to lose her virginity up against the Co-op wall? There was nothing romantic in view at all – only puddles and the special offer posters in the Co-op window.

She felt the metal button on her jeans slip through the eyelet, and caught a glimpse of his greedy face. He pushed his hand down though the zip was only half undone. It crushed into her abdomen, his fingers scraped through her pubic hair.

'No!' With one huge push she threw him off balance and in the moment before his brain caught up, Zee had wriggled free. 'You bastard!'

He looked at her, dazed. 'What's the matter with you?'

'You *know* what's the matter. You should have stopped when I told you to.'

'You think I can? Just like that?'

'You'd better learn to – or you'll end up in prison!'

'What did you think we were going to do?'

'I didn't want to do anything!'

'You were up for it, you slag! You know you were.'

'You only think that 'cos you keep your brains in your balls, Des Gordon.'

'You frigid wee hoor! What's wrong with you?'

Later, she would laugh about that particular insult but just then it brought tears to her eyes. 'Tasha?' she called half heartedly across the pitch. 'Tasha?'

'Leave her,' Des grunted.

'She's to come home with me.'

'She's screwing, you daft cow.'

'No, she isn't!' Zee heard her voice wobbling. She didn't want to desert Tasha. She didn't want to believe Des.

'Aye, she is. Gary always gets what *he* wants.'

There was something so jealous in Des's voice that it made Zee shiver. She walked shakily around to the other side of the Co-op. There was no sign of Tasha and it was almost five to twelve.

Was Des right after all? Where was Tasha? What was she doing? She seemed so much more experienced than Zee was. It made her feel even worse, such a *child*.

Tasha and Gary were having sex, of course they were. Hadn't tonight been all Tasha's idea? The alcohol, then meeting up with the crowd? Tasha had known exactly what she wanted. Maybe it was her, Zee, who was odd, for not wanting sex. Frigid, weird . . . just like Des said.

She started walking up the pavement where a few hours earlier they had played hopscotch. Des's words banged like a drumbeat around her head.

'You were up for it, you slag...You frigid wee hoor...What's wrong with you?...frigid wee hoor... what's wrong...?'

She started sobbing; she couldn't help it. Desperate for home, she broke into a run.

7

When Tasha woke up the following morning, her pillow was damp with tears. Her head ached and her body felt like a dead weight. When she managed to heave herself into a sitting position, every bone and muscle hurt. She soaked in a deep foamy bath but even that barely helped.

In the mirror some creature with limp hair and skin like potato peel stared back at her. The creature's eyes were blank. How could she ever get her head round what had happened to her last night? How could she face anyone if she couldn't face herself? She tried to watch television but couldn't concentrate. Music messed her head up even more. She spent forty minutes screwing up the courage to ring Zee. If Gary answered she could hang up, couldn't she?

Her hand hovered, trembling, over the dial pad and the receiver made her palm sweat. She tapped in the digits with her heart pounding then jumped when the phone pealed out shrilly at the other end...three... five...seven...nine times...pick it up, Zee, *please* pick it up...but there was no answer. Distraught, Tasha burst into tears.

She went downstairs about eleven o'clock, knowing she had better put in an appearance.

'I lay awake waiting for you last night,' snapped her mum. 'Do you know what time you came in?'

'Sorry, I lost track of the time.' Tasha scooted outside to the garden but her mother followed her.

'It was after half past twelve,' she went on. 'That's twice in one week!'

Big deal, thought Tasha, but she apologised again.

'How did you lose track of the time? You've got a watch.'

'I wasn't wearing it.'

'Well, why not?'

'It didn't match my top.'

'Tasha!'

This time last year, she might have confided in her mum, but not now and certainly not when she was in a mood. Tasha's head rattled. She had never had a hangover before and she wished her mother would stop shouting, stop going on and on about safety and thoughtlessness and good manners. The only thing that really stuck in Tasha's aching brain was her mum talking about herself and Miguel as an item all the time.

'Look, I'm trying to be reasonable,' she was saying now, 'but we've got to be able to trust you.'

'We?' said Tasha before she could stop herself. 'Miguel isn't my dad.'

'But he is my husband.'

'So?'

'So it wouldn't hurt you to be a bit more friendly towards him.'

'He wasn't being very friendly to me last night! What I wear's got nothing to do with him.'

'Miguel's a human being, Tasha, not some sort of

robot. He's got opinions and he's entitled to voice them. Just for the record, your own dad wouldn't have wanted you going out dressed like that either. Nor did I.'

'You just want to spoil my fun.'

'Rubbish. Being dressed like that's an invitation...'

'To what?'

'You *know* what. It's irresponsible. We're glad you enjoyed yourself – of course we are – but you've got to come home on time. We've *got* to be able to trust you.'

Tears flooded into Tasha's eyes and she turned away. She couldn't handle this conversation. *Enjoyed herself*? *Trust*? If they only knew...

'Are you all right?' her mother asked suddenly. 'You don't seem quite yourself this morning.'

Tasha knew that this was her chance to speak, but how could she? Where would she begin? How could she explain the alcohol, Gary, her own stupidity? Her mother would kill her. Miguel would be convinced that she really was the slut he already suspected. They would probably send her packing and that would mean back to school because her own father couldn't find time for her...

'I'm okay. I'll wear my watch in future, yeah?'

She sat down on the grass beside a tortoiseshell cat washing its face with its paws and her mother went back indoors. The cat tiptoed onto Tasha's lap and looked up at her with calm round eyes. She cuddled it close and it purred with happiness, its hot, comforting fur mopping up her tears.

Later, as a peace offering, she made Miguel a mug of

strong sweet coffee, just the way he liked it. He thanked her solemnly and her mother beamed. If it kept them off her back, thought Tasha, it was worth it.

She spent most of the day alone and late that afternoon, when Zee called, she found her fast asleep on her bed.

'Whatever's wrong?' she asked at once. 'You look awful.'

'Oh, Zee,' she said, then found that she couldn't say any more. She wanted to. She had to tell somebody and she had thought it would be easy to tell Zee, but it wasn't. She felt so incredibly stupid that it wasn't going to be easy to tell anyone.

'Is it something I did?' asked Zee. 'I'm sorry I didn't wait last night but I couldn't – not any longer.'

'It's not you – it's *me*.' Tears scalded Tasha's cheeks. 'I've been so...so stupid, Zee.'

'No...oh my God, you haven't...have you?'

Tasha nodded and whispered, 'With your brother.'

'Right.' Zee's face paled in front of her. 'Gary didn't...he didn't...?'

'Rape me?' She shook her head. 'The truth is that I... wanted him to...but not like *that*.'

'What do you mean?'

'He was so *callous*.' She shook her head violently, sending tears flying. 'I don't think he even knew who he was screwing, Zee.'

'Of course he did. Anyone can see Gary likes you.'

'Then why did he hurt me? He hurt me a lot, Zee.'

'I'm so sorry.'

74

'It's not your fault. It should have been special but it wasn't special at all. It was horrible. It felt cheap. *I* felt cheap, like a ... like a slut.'

Zee put her arms around her and gave her a hug. 'You poor thing. Des was awful last night. The same thing *almost* happened to me.'

Tasha listened to Zee's story in silence but nothing could change what had happened. 'The big difference,' she pointed out afterwards, 'is that it didn't happen to you because you stopped it.'

'I didn't fancy Des, otherwise, who knows? Maybe I would have. Don't you think *I* want to know what it's like too?'

'You're missing nothing!' said Tasha bitterly. 'Afterwards, Gary wanted me to go to a party one of the crowd was throwing. Can you believe that? As if nothing had happened. As if I was some cheap little tart who screws around every Saturday night. I couldn't face it, Zee.'

'I hope the rat walked you home?'

Tasha nodded. 'I thought he'd go home too, but no. He said he was going to the party anyway.' She wiped her eyes with a tissue that Zee gave her. 'I expect he went back to Ruby Mason.'

'Do you really think so?'

'He was with her earlier, wasn't he? And I know she went to the party because he told us so! To think of him going back to *her* moments after we'd ... '

'Tasha.' Zee blushed and seemed to force herself to go on. 'Did you ... did Gary ... use anything ... like a condom?'

Tasha shook her head and more tears leaked out. It felt as if they would never stop now. 'No,' she whispered. 'I've been going mad here, worrying.' There had been nothing, no mention of contraception, precious little conversation at all, in fact, and certainly no condom. 'Oh, Zee, how could I have been so stupid?'

'I'll kill him, I swear, I'll kill Gary!'

'Never mind *him*, what if I'm pregnant? What will I do?'

'It won't come to that.' Suddenly Zee was matter-of-fact and practical. 'We've got to get you the morning after pill. Damn! The chemists will be closed now and tomorrow's Sunday.'

'Whatever are you talking about?'

'Emergency contraception – to stop you falling pregnant.'

A bolt of excitement and hope shot through Tasha. This seemed almost too good to be true. 'How can it do that? I mean, when I've already had sex? Isn't it too late?'

'Not yet. You have to take it within seventy-two hours. Haven't they taught you this at school?'

'They never teach us anything this useful.'

'Emergency contraception stops a fertilised egg planting itself in your womb.'

'Really? How wonderful!'

Zee frowned; she was obviously making a huge effort to remember. 'They said it makes the lining of the womb inhospitable. It's not the same as an abortion – it just stops it all happening. That's why it's called emergency contraception. You *could* actually wait until Monday and get it then from a chemist.'

'I'll go mad worrying meantime.'

Zee nodded sympathetically. 'The only other way is to see a doctor.'

'But I haven't got a doctor!' cried Tasha, panicking. 'Not here in Belfast. Besides, I'm under age – I'm only fifteen.'

'There's a special clinic for young people somewhere in Belfast – you can get it there. It's free. Oh... what's the name of the place?'

'For God's sake, think!'

'I know – Yellow Pages.'

Ten minutes and one phonecall later they had the address. The clinic was only open for another hour and a half.

Zee's brain seemed to have gone into overdrive. 'We can't hang around for a bus, we'll have to ring a taxi. How much money have you got?'

Tasha shook her head frantically. Her entire allowance had gone on make-up. 'Can't we ask your mum for a loan, Zee?'

'No way, she has no spare money. What about your mum?'

'Daren't risk it. I'm already in her bad books. If they find out about this, I'm dead.'

Tears started tumbling down her face again. She felt so helpless, so foolish, so totally out of her depth.

'I know,' said Zee calmly. 'We'll ask Conor.'

'Conor?'

'He'll lend us cash.' Zee gritted her teeth. 'He'd *better*.'

8

As they hurried up the O'Keefes' short stony drive, Mrs Gordon peered at them over her neat garden hedge.

'Look at Des's mum,' muttered Zee, 'she's practically panting with curiosity. You'd think she'd have the decency to spy on people from behind her net curtains at least.'

'They *are* in,' Mrs Gordon called out reedily.

'Well they're not hearing us,' retorted Zee and she knocked again.

'Sure they'll be at their tea at this time of day. They have an early tea, you know. Their kitchen's round the back.'

Zee lowered her voice. 'I bet she knows what time they empty their bowels too.'

'Could I maybe help you, girls?'

Tasha and Zee looked at each other and started giggling. It was Tasha who recovered first. 'I don't think so, Mrs Gordon, but thank you for offering.'

'That's quite all right, m'dear. I hear your father... er ...Mr Mo-whatsi...is rather famous. A musician? I appreciate a nice bit of Bach myself.' She cleared her throat and pulled at the collar of her flowery apron. ' Ahem! Zara, young lady, you should mind your manners – you've not introduced us yet.'

'Sorry, but we're kinda pushed for time,' said Zee.

Mrs G's eyes narrowed; she was not easily deterred. Crooking her forefinger, she beckoned to Tasha who went to the hedge obediently while Zee continued knocking.

'Hello, Mrs Gordon. I'm Natasha – I'm pleased to meet you.'

'Oh...what beautiful manners...and such *lovely* teeth.' Mrs Gordon expelled a long satisfied sigh as Tasha smiled, treating her to another dazzling display of polished enamel. Mrs Gordon lowered her voice. 'I feel it's only fair to warn you, m'dear...you be careful of that one there.'

'Who? Zee?'

'I believe that's what she calls herself.' Mrs G sniffed disdainfully. 'Though why anyone should want to shorten their name when they've had the honour of being called after royalty defeats me. Does it not you? An insult to the Princess Royal, that's what it is.'

Tasha felt another giggle building, in spite of her own desperate situation. 'Perhaps Princess Anne won't find out,' she whispered conspiratorially. 'And Zee's awfully nice – honestly.'

Mrs Gordon's drawstring lips disappeared inside her mouth and the steely hairs on the end of her chin stood to attention. 'Tragedy's wrecked that family so it has. The boy's gone wild and the mother hardly moves beyond that garden of hers. As for thon wee girl, well!'

'Well what...?' asked Tasha in surprise.

'I fear for her, so I do.'

'Fear for her?'

'Aye, for her moral safety.'

Tasha only just managed to turn her hysteria into a boneshaker of a coughing fit. 'Why's that?' she spluttered.

'This is the second time in a fortnight I've seen her at the O'Keefes' door.'

'Is there some reason she shouldn't visit the O'Keefes?'

Indecision kneaded Mrs Gordon's round grey face like a pound of pastry. 'It's really not for me to say...' she muttered. 'I mean, *I'm* no gossip.'

'No, of course not... I'd better get back to Zee then...'

'On the other hand... you being a stranger... maybe you need to know our ways – for your own good, of course.'

'Of course. You were saying...'

'I've nothing against them myself, no, nothing at all. But young Zara there – she should have more sense. Stick to her own kind... especially after what her family's been through. There's no knowing what young Gary would do if he thought she was dilly-dallying with one of them.'

'One of them? With a Catholic, you mean?'

'Exactly. Don't get me wrong, m'dear. I'm all for peace – of course I am – just so long as they keep their distance. Know what I mean?'

Tasha was beginning to understand. 'My mother,' she replied thoughtfully, 'and Miguel say that prejudice is always wrong.'

'So it is!' Mrs Gordon nodded emphatically. 'Sure we

80

all think that – but you have to use a bit of common sense at the same time.'

The old hypocrite was starting to irritate Tasha and she was relieved when Zee shouted to her.

'Come on, Tash! I'm fed up standing here.'

'Go round the back,' urged Mrs Gordon. 'Have I not told you the once?'

'I've never met anyone like her,' Tasha whispered as they crunched across the gravel.

'Lucky you. Northern Ireland's full of Mrs Gs.'

They walked around the side of the house past a big square kitchen window which it was impossible not to look through. Sure enough the whole O'Keefe clan was assembled there, all ten of them sitting at a long table eating strawberries. Twenty brown eyes fastened on the girls like laser beams.

Mrs O'Keefe opened the back door just as they reached it. She was dark haired and the fine lines around her eyes and mouth reminded Zee of hill markings on an ordinance survey map. Her hands were thick and red from heaving coal buckets and doing the washing up. Zee thought she looked just like a Catholic and she was ashamed of herself for thinking it.

'What can I do for you?' Mrs O'Keefe asked, smiling at them.

'It's Conor we've come to see,' said Zee.

They heard a wave of teasing inside, then Mr O'Keefe shouted out to them. 'Come back later, girls, can you not see we're eating?'

Zee's heart pounded. He sounded scary but there just

wasn't time to wait. 'I'm sorry,' she called back. 'But it's urgent.'

There was more teasing, then Conor's mum smiled again.

'Pay no notice to that rabble,' she said. 'Come on in, girls.'

Conor wasn't hard to pick out at the table because he had a face like a flamingo. His brothers were having a great time.

'You're a dark horse, Con.'

'Not one girl, but two!'

'Be quiet, you eejits!' barked Conor.

Only the youngest two children, seated on either side of their father, had more important things on their minds.

'You've had seven strawberries already, Diarmaid!' said one.

'So have you.'

'But I'm a year bigger than you. I *need* more.'

'That's not—'

'Quiet!' bawled Mr O'Keefe. 'If you're going to fight, we'll give the last strawberry to our new neighbour here.'

The two kids looked mutinous as he held aloft a white dinner plate with a single jewel-like berry. Tasha froze, but Zee giggled. She thought the whole scene looked like something out of *Oliver Twist*. Promptly, she grabbed a knife from the table and sliced the plump berry in two.

'There! Enough for the both of them!'

Mrs O'Keefe laughed. 'By heaven, Zee, they should

have you in the peace process. Conor, take the girls through the house – you'll get privacy in the parlour.'

Mr O'Keefe looked as if he would much rather they didn't have privacy and his bald head seemed to shimmer with curiosity. As for Conor, he looked as if he would rather evaporate than move, but he got up eventually and led them through the house in silence.

'I'm sorry,' Zee blurted as soon as he had shut the parlour door.

'You're not half one for surprises,' he said.

'I didn't mean to turn up like this but it's an emergency – and you did say you'd help me.'

'Are you all right? What's happened?'

'Nothing. We just need some money, Con, that's all.'

'Money?' he repeated.

'A fiver.' She hesitated. 'Maybe a tenner?'

'What the hell for?'

He looked thunderous and Zee began to wonder if this had been such a good idea after all. She glanced at Tasha but she was looking away. 'The thing is ... I've called a taxi but we haven't got the money to pay for it.'

'Well then, you have got a problem.' Conor crossed his arms unsympathetically.

'You said you'd help me!'

'And maybe I will – *when* I know what it's for.'

'Oh, tell him!' cried Tasha, spinning round. 'Just tell him, Zee.'

'Tell me what?'

There was silence.

'I need the morning after pill,' blurted Tasha. 'We

haven't got a bean to pay for the taxi and the clinic shuts in forty-five minutes.'

Conor stared at Tasha, then he stared at Zee. His eyes were growing rounder by the moment. 'Right,' he said at last, 'we'd better get a move on then.'

'*We*?' Zee felt her face light up, she couldn't help it. 'You're coming too, Conor?'

'Sure.' He grinned at her. 'Call it my good deed for the day if you like.'

They made for the front door. Conor grabbed his jacket off a peg and shouted to his parents. 'I'm heading out – see you later.'

At that the kitchen door burst open and Mr O'Keefe came hurrying through. 'Out where?' he demanded.

'Just out,' replied Conor, 'I'll be back in a couple of hours.'

'I wanted a hand in the garage, son.'

'Get one of the others to help you, Dad.'

'But Conor—'

'What?'

Mr O'Keefe's nostrils flared as he looked the girls over suspiciously. 'What's going on, Conor?'

'Nothing. The girls are friends, that's all.' Conor stared back boldly at his father. 'Have you got a problem with that?'

9

The taxi driver swerved like a bull-fighter, racing between the lanes of traffic clogging up the Ormeau Road.

'We're all gonna die!' giggled Zee, clutching Conor's arm.

'Relax,' he said, grinning at her. 'We'll get there.'

Watching them, Tasha wondered if it was all some awful dream. She sensed that, despite her own predicament, Zee and Conor were actually enjoying themselves.

'Are you okay?' Zee asked a moment later, her voice tinged with guilt.

'Do you think this clinic is going to be some dreadful seedy place,' murmured Tasha, 'with prostitutes hanging around outside it and syringes on the ground?'

'Why on earth should it be?' asked Zee.

'Bet it is,' mumbled Conor, 'bet it's stuck up some stinking alley.'

'Bet it *isn't*.' Zee glared at him.

'What does it matter,' he persisted, 'as long as Tasha gets what she wants?'

But it did matter and Tasha could feel tears burning behind her eyes. 'What if they think I'm a slut, Zee? What if they make me *feel* like one?'

'Call it a steep learning curve,' muttered Conor.

'Shut up you!' Zee gave Tasha's arm a reassuring squeeze and tossed Conor a look that would have frozen acid. As the taxi braked, they all lurched sideways, collapsing on each other like playing cards. 'We're here,' said Zee, pointing, 'and look – it isn't seedy at all.'

The waiting room was large and comfortable with modern furniture and pastel painted walls. It was filled with young people about their own age. Some had spiky haircuts and nose-rings, some wore slick make-up and smart skirts but most looked in between, jeans-and-jerseys sort of people like themselves. There was a murmur of conversation and folk were reading magazines, or the leaflets that lay about on polished pine tables, describing different kinds of contraception. Pop music gave the place a buzz.

'Hi,' said a receptionist with a friendly smile. 'You're new clients, aren't you? I'll have to take a few details.'

'Whatever for?' demanded Tasha nervously. 'I thought these places were confidential. Will my mother find out I've been here?'

'No. It is *absolutely* confidential.'

'Even if I'm under sixteen?'

'Yes. Everyone's entitled to confidentiality – whatever their age. But we do need details. That way, next time you come, we can look up your notes, see what we've done before and work out the best way to help you.'

'I won't *be* back,' vowed Tasha.

The receptionist grinned again. 'Sounds like you've got a lot on your mind. Fancy a chat with Rose, our counsellor? She could take your details when you're feeling more relaxed and then you can see the doctor.'

'I-I'm not sure,' said Tasha. 'I just need the

morning after pill. A counsellor's for people with problems, isn't it?'

'It's for anyone who feels a chat might help,' said a young woman getting up from behind a desk. She had waist length black hair, tight jeans and an embroidered waistcoat. 'I'm Rose, by the way.'

'She doesn't looks too bad,' whispered Zee.

Tasha thought so too. In fact she looked really friendly.

'I was just about to make some tea,' added Rose. 'Fancy a cup?'

Tasha took a deep breath. 'Okay.' She turned to the others. 'You needn't wait. I'll get a bus home. Thanks for getting me this far.'

'I'll wait if you want me to,' said Zee earnestly.

'Honestly, there's no need.'

'Then I'll come over tonight, I promise.'

'Good luck,' muttered Conor and he threw her a wink as he legged it towards the door.

'Milk and sugar?' asked Rose.

The room they went to had *Counsellor* printed formally on the door but inside there were pictures of rolling farmlands on the walls and a bowl of sweet smelling roses stood on a coffee table. Tasha half expected Rose to direct her to the big desk in the corner. Not that Rose looked at all teachery. Instead she waved her towards a big brown armchair with soft cushions.

'That's the most comfortable seat,' she said. 'Make yourself at home. And remember, nothing you say in here goes beyond these four walls.'

'Um . . . right.' Tasha sipped self-consciously at her tea

while Rose plonked herself down in the chair opposite.

'Were those folk at reception good friends of yours?' she asked.

'Zee is. If it wasn't for her I don't know what I'd have done today.'

'How come?'

'She brought me here. I didn't even know the morning after pill existed until she told me.'

Rose's brown eyes were grave. 'You didn't know it existed but you had unprotected sex anyway?'

'Um...' Tasha hadn't expected such plain speaking somehow. Unprotected sex. It sounded so...careless. To her horror, her eyes filled up with tears again. Rose indicated a box of tissues on the coffee table.

'Cry all you want to. We get through tons of tissues here.' She was not embarrassed by the crying, and she didn't try to comfort Tasha. She just waited as if Tasha's tears were completely necessary and useful. 'Feel any better?' she asked afterwards.

'Maybe – I'm not sure.'

'So, it was unprotected sex, yeah?'

'Yes – but only because I was drunk. I wouldn't have done it otherwise.'

'Drink generally disinhibits people.'

'What?'

'It gives them false courage – and makes them do things they wouldn't do sober.'

Tasha swallowed the huge lump that rose up in her throat. If only she could stop feeling so stupid.

'I did rather wonder if it *might* happen – even before I

went out last night – but I'd never have gone through with it if I hadn't been drunk. What a mess.' She raked her hand through her hair despairingly. 'I'll never drink again!'

'I doubt that, but you should certainly aim for responsible drinking,' said Rose gently and she sipped her tea which gave Tasha a few moments to collect herself.

'It sounds as if there were other reasons you had sex, Tasha? Apart from the booze?'

'Well, Gary's seriously good looking. I couldn't believe it when I realised he fancied me.'

'Why not? Why couldn't you believe it?'

Rose was sharp but there was no going back now.

'No one else ever has,' said Tasha quietly.

'I find that hard to believe.'

'Do you? The thing is...I go to this posh boarding school.'

'Aah. Where they protect your virtue?'

'Like nuns! The headmistress even thinks going to church on Sunday is a bit risky.'

'Afraid of affairs in the vestry, is she?'

Tasha laughed. Who would have believed that a stranger could be so easy to talk to? 'Mind you,' she confided, 'some of the girls are so desperate they'd probably settle for the verger! I mean, sex is all we ever talk about at school.'

'So you felt really excited when Gary showed an interest?'

'Yes!'

'And you wanted to get close to him?'

'Yeah – specially as nobody else can.'

Rose frowned. 'I don't understand. Why can't anyone else get close to him?'

'Gary's sort of closed off, complicated – he's Zee's brother – he's been like that ever since their dad died. He got murdered, you see.' She stopped because her voice was slithering about like raindrops on a window pane. 'But *I* know what it feels like to be lonely too.'

'Take your time,' said Rose gently.

'I wanted to share all that with Gary. Talk to him about it, so he'd know he wasn't the only one. Show him that we'd be good together.'

'And Gary?'

'What about him?'

'What did you think Gary wanted?'

Tasha stared at her. 'I didn't *think*,' she blurted, realising it for the first time. 'I just assumed he'd want the same thing as me.'

'And what do you think now, Tasha?'

'Huh, he was only after sex.'

There was a pause. 'Did Gary force you to have sex?'

'No. I wanted... I wanted to find out... you know... what it's like. But I didn't think it was the *only* thing he was interested in.' The humiliation smouldering inside her like an abandoned bonfire burst alight again. Rose waited patiently until her tears stopped.

'It sounds as if you thought sex would make you feel good for all sorts of reasons, Tasha. You were curious about it, you were lonely, you fancied Gary and you wanted to help him.'

'I hadn't thought it out that clearly.' Tasha smiled ruefully. 'It doesn't sound quite so sordid put like that.'

'Is sordid still how it feels?'

Tasha nodded and whispered, 'It happened on a football pitch. I feel so ashamed...so dirty. A *football pitch*. I mean, that can't be normal?'

'Listen, you didn't do anything abnormal. Unfortunate, yes, but not abnormal. And your reaction is completely normal.'

'Really?'

'Yes – really!'

Rose's sympathy was so genuine, so focused, that it was a kind of release. 'I'm *not* a slut,' said Tasha fiercely.

'Of course you're not. You made a mistake – we're allowed to make mistakes. We're all human. It's learning from them that's important.'

Tasha groaned. 'And I have an awful lot to learn, haven't I?'

'Perhaps. It sounds to me as if you and Gary just weren't communicating.'

'We weren't even talking!'

'But in future...'

'I'll communicate, believe me.'

'Good. Maybe, you should spend some time thinking about what you actually want from a relationship – from any relationship.'

'Okay.'

'And think about how you approach a boy. How you talk to him? The kind of signals you send out?'

'You're awfully diplomatic. You mean, don't fling myself at men, don't you?'

'And, before it gets physical, *do* think about contraception.'

'Don't worry, I will.' Tasha smiled at the counsellor. 'When I came in here I just wanted to grab that tablet and run, but I'm glad we've talked now.'

Rose grinned back. 'Were you scared of what might come out?'

'Maybe. I don't usually talk to adults – not any more.'

'What about your parents?'

'I don't see much of my dad. My mum's just remarried – this Bosnian guy who's a bit weird. Sometimes they even talk Serbo-Croat...' she fizzled out crossly.

'Sounds like you've got a lot on your plate.'

'Yeah, I have! No one else seems to realise it though.'

'So how does that make you feel?'

'Alone.' She was surprised how quickly the word spilled out as if it had been sitting there just inside her mouth for months. 'Yeah, alone.'

'Anything else, Tasha?'

'A bit... betrayed. I know it's stupid but I never thought about Mum marrying again. I just wish she'd asked me first. And I wish I'd had a chance to get to know Miguel before they married.'

'Are you going to tell your mum this?'

'She doesn't want to hear stuff like that. She just wants us all to get on.'

'Maybe you're frightened that telling her will push

you further apart?'

'Yeah, maybe I am.'

They sat quietly for a few moments absorbing things, then Rose said, 'Of course, it might give you a chance to work things out together.'

'It might, but it's risky, isn't it? Mum might be angry with me.'

'Is that likely?'

'No.'

'Life's full of risks, Tasha, and responsibilities.'

'Maybe I should just get on with things – you know – put up and shut up.'

'It is one option and things might well work out eventually. But it will take far longer and until then you will go on feeling alone and betrayed. And *that* can create other problems, can't it?'

'Like Gary,' said Tasha. She was beginning, dully, to make connections.

'Talking of Gary, what do you want to do about him? Are you going to tell him how you feel?'

Tasha shuddered. Gary's eyes had been as hard as icicles as he pushed his way inside her. Sharp ridges of earth had grazed her back. When she cried out he ignored her. She had lain still then, pinned down, gasping with shock. Intimacy was what she had longed for but it had just been sex. Cold, insulting sex. Gary had turned her into his toy and she had felt like some rag-doll prostitute. He had finished with a final clutching groan and rolled off her to swig lager from a can.

'I don't want Gary anywhere near me,' she said firmly. '*Ever* again.'

Rose opened her mouth, then she closed it again without speaking. Tasha thought that when the counsellor smiled at her this time, she looked rather sad.

Outside the clinic, Zee and Conor hung about uncertainly. Zee was hardly ever at a loss for words but the easy banter in the taxi had vanished now they were alone. Conor, teetering on the kerb with his hands in his pockets, looked just as uncomfortable.

'Maybe we should take Gary home a wee present from the clinic,' he said.

'What do you mean?' asked Zee.

'A free goodie bag. They're very discreet, you know.'

He meant condoms, she realised with a jolt. 'Do you come here often then?' she asked, determined to embarrass him back. 'You seem to know an awful lot about it.'

'So it was Gary who had his wicked way with Tasha? Ha!'

'I'm not saying that.'

'You don't need to. Sure Tasha was all over him on the eleventh night.'

There was no denying that. Zee sighed. 'I don't think she's going to be asking for a goodie bag today, anyway.'

After another awkward silence, Conor said, 'C'mon, I'd better take you home then.'

'Take me?' Zee's temper came up fast. 'What am I? Some sort of puppy? I don't come with a lead attached, you know.'

'You snap like a puppy,' he retorted.

She stuck out her tongue at him and wished instantly she hadn't. What age was she for heaven's sake? What was she doing here alone with him anyway? Just when she'd got her head straight, here he was, scrambling all her good intentions.

'What I meant,' he said sourly, 'was, would you like to go home, Zee?'

She knew she should but instead she said, 'We've only just escaped Hazel Grove, haven't we?'

'Coffee, then?'

Panic sprinted down her spine. Coffee meant tables for two, soft music, candles. It was all happening too fast. She had to keep control of things. 'We could hang out in the shopping mall,' she suggested. 'By the fountain or something.'

'I *hate* shopping malls,' he said.

'Oh. Gary hates them too.'

'So he and I have something in common after all?'

'Aye, shopping malls and a tendency to wind people up.'

'Me?' Conor looked offended. 'Dunno know what you mean.'

'Liar. Didn't you think Tasha was having a bad enough day? What got into you, stirring it up like that in the taxi?'

'Sorry.'

'It's Tasha you should apologise to,' she said tartly.

'I will.' He sighed. 'Would you rather I hadn't come?'

'No!' She felt a rush of warmth towards Conor and

her cheeks tingled. 'I'm really glad you came. I thought you were dead brave standing up to your dad too. He doesn't want you anywhere near me, does he?'

'I only told him the truth.'

'How d'you mean?'

'Well, we are just friends ... aren't we?'

Their eyes collided like cars and her stomach felt as if it had been punctured by flying metal. She spun on her heel and started walking fast.

'So where are we off to?' asked Conor, falling into step beside her.

'The docks. I love it there – I go quite often.'

'A nice girl like you?'

She laughed and he put his arm around her waist, and Zee took one huge breath and put her arm around him. She felt thrilled, almost dizzy, as they walked through the streets. Strangers passing them by would assume they were a couple.

It wasn't far to the docks. Old undeveloped dockland, not the fashionable, fling-away-a-fortune apartment area for rich folk who wanted the whole world to know they had finally arrived.

Arm in arm they walked, the shifting smells of oil and rope and salt rippling over them, mixed up with the smells of fish and rain and diesel. Old dockland had a charm all its own. The narrow streets were cobble-stoned and dusty. Ramshackle cottages that had once housed whole families leaned into each other now, their windows boarded up. They had long since been vacated and now they were only used as sheds. Outsized padlocks hanging on the doors radiated messages of crime. At night the dark streets would swarm with prostitutes and drunks.

'Fantastic, isn't it?' said Zee as they crossed a concrete wharf. 'You can smell the excitement.'

'All I can smell's the pollution,' said Conor.

It was noisy too. Cranes, dump-trucks and fork-lifts were busy shifting boxes of cargo. Men with clip-boards and hard hats shouted instructions. Engines stopped and started. Horns blared. They were loading a black and white Scandinavian ship registered in Stockholm. Thick steel ropes lay coiled at the ready, orange canvases were pinned firmly down and the blue deck was still glistening from being scrubbed.

'Smart outfit,' remarked Conor and smoke belched self importantly from the black and white funnel.

'I think she's agreeing with you,' laughed Zee. She caught his arm. 'Look! There's the ferry for Liverpool.'

They walked round to it, dwarfed by its high sides and the rows of portholes stretching in front of them and way behind. Zee peered down into the oily water under the gangway and shivered. 'I wouldn't fancy falling in there.'

'Sure I'd come to your rescue – I'd swing down that rope with a box of Milk Tray in me hand.'

'Eejit! Sometimes I do think about doing a bunk,' she confided. 'Stowing myself away and going to London. I could be office dogsbody on a newspaper. Does that sound daft?'

'Yeah, it does,' he said.

It wasn't the answer she had wanted somehow. She let go of his arm and pushed him away playfully.

'Would you really go off and leave your whole family, Zee?'

'Everyone has to take the plunge sometime.'

'Aye, but we don't all go across the water.'

'It's only the Irish sea, not the Atlantic. England's not far.'

Sometimes she did wonder how she would cope, then she imagined the relief of living without her mum's sadness and Gary's moods, poised above her like big black clouds.

'There's a whole world out there, Con. I'm gonna go places, do things, meet people!'

'Send us a postcard then, won't you?'

Suddenly he was irritating her. 'What is it with you, Con? Do you want to be stuck in this backwater for the rest of your life? Listening to politicians bicker on the radio?' She jerked an imaginary microphone up to her mouth. 'So is there peace or isn't there, Mr Adams? When is a beating not a beating? When is a riot a riot?' She dropped her hand in disgust. 'They don't know if they're coming or going. They're all nuts! What's there to stay for?'

'I want to live where I can do some good,' said Conor. 'How's Ireland ever going to change if all the decent folk leave? Tell me that.'

'Do you think I care? Look what happened to my dad. I'm not going to stick around and watch that happen to one of my kids in a few years' time.'

'Shush up, Zee.'

'What do you mean, shush!'

Conor turned and held her gently by the shoulders. 'The last thing I want to do is argue. I want to make the most of you while I can.'

She stared at him. Her emotions felt about as stable as a wave on a beach. One part of her wanted to surge towards him, another part was sucking her back. 'As long as you realise,' she started, 'that I'm...I'm not going to be in Belfast for long and—'

'Shush,' he said again.

'But—'

'I really like you, Zee, I can't get you out of my head.'

'It'll have to be secret,' she blurted. 'Otherwise Ga—'

'No four lettered words,' he said.

'But we need to talk.'

'No, not just now we don't.'

He cradled her face between his hands. 'Girl with the laughing eyes,' he said. 'That's how I've always thought of you. I never really believed I'd get the chance to tell you so.'

'Always? You mean ... '

'Have I fancied you from afar? Yeah...forever I think.'

Words seemed to be sucked away from her. Thoughts vanished too and all she was left with were her feelings. It felt scary and magical and weird all at once. Zee Proctor, was this really happening to her? She had been out once or twice with boys before but it had never felt like this. Not this bellyache of excitement, not this longing like a sickness, not this disbelief, the whole lot shaken about as if she was on a fairground waltzer, and laced with that same intoxicating fear.

So different from how she had felt with Des. The wind whipped Conor's hair back from his shy eyes. They were the colour of shiny new chestnuts and as soft as pools. Deep enough to drown in, wasn't that what people said?

They brushed lips and he kissed her nose, her cheeks, her forehead. When she smiled he pulled her gently towards him and her lips searched again for his. Their arms closed around each other in a circle and suddenly the wind was dancing around them, not between.

The cranes, dump-trucks and fork-lifts carried on as normal and the Liverpool ferry hooted and sailed away.

10

The afternoon heat welded Gary's shirt to his back. Before him stretched the Newtownards Road and in the distance towered Belfast shipyard's two huge cranes, Samson and Delilah. 'Slow down, Des!' he gasped. 'I'm sweating like a racehorse here.'

'More like a bloody donkey.' Des eyed Gary's thick winter jacket with disgust. 'Fancy wearing a donkey jacket when it's seventy-five degrees.'

'I needed pockets, didn't I?' Gary's fingers trembled around the brown paper parcel in his pocket. 'Don't know why you can't carry this thing – it was all your idea.'

'Because you're less likely to get lifted,' snapped Des. 'Why didn't you use a sports bag, dumbo? Nothing like making yourself conspicuous.'

'D'you really think the RUC wouldn't bother searching mc?'

''Course. There isn't a policeman in Belfast who didn't know your dad, is there? Drop his name into the conversation and they'd soon leave you in peace.'

Gary wasn't so sure but Des was off on one of his rants again.

'Do you remember the time we were in his patrol car and he got called to that bank robbery?'

'Of course I do.'

'We must have done ninety that day!' Des laughed.

'And when we got there he just pulled his gun and went straight in. Mr Cool or what?'

'There was back up,' said Gary.

'Aye, but he was The Man. When he came back out with those two robbers, do you remember how everyone cheered?'

Gary could recall every detail. The flashing blue lights, the radios crackling, even the stains on the paving stones he had stared at, willing his dad to reappear. And Jack Proctor had come back – that time.

'What a hero!' shouted Des. 'He stopped those Fenian gits. He knew he had to and *we're* just doing the same thing.'

'I don't think he'd see it that way.' Gary was feeling less and less sure of this plan. He took off his jacket and slung it over his shoulder and the weight of the package pulled it to one side. 'I wish I knew what was in this thing,' he muttered.

'We're nearly there.'

The rendezvous point was in a park edged with roses. There were folk sunbathing, a sweaty jogger and mothers pushing buggies. They were to wait at the third bench on the left-hand side of the pond. At least that was vacant, thought Gary, but there was no sign of the two men they were supposed to meet.

'Where the hell are they?' he said nervously.

'Stop panicking – they'll be here.'

Gary folded his jacket and put it down carefully on the bench. Then he took out a hanky and wiped his face. The sweat soaked it through at once.

'We should have brought some cans,' said Des lightly. 'Had ourselves a picnic.'

'Have you ever tried running when you're pissed?' retorted Gary.

'Will you chill out? We won't have to run, everything's going to be fine.'

Gary tried a shrug but his shoulders were too tense. 'Jimmy and Ben give me the creeps,' he said, remembering when Des had introduced them in a pub. 'Especially that Ben – he's a real headbanger.'

'It's cash in hand remember. Just you leave everything to your Uncle Des.'

Gary was about to put Des in his place when he noticed a group of teenagers in the distance. There must have been fifteen of them. They were too far away to pick out individually but he recognised the two who detached themselves and started walking towards them.

'Jeezus, no! It's Tasha and Zee. What are they doing here?'

'Calm down. Jimmy and Ben won't come near us if they see them.'

'I hope not,' spluttered Gary.

Des raised his arm and shouted. 'Fancy meeting you here!'

'I knew something would go wrong.'

'Will you stop worrying? You've been trying to speak to Tasha all week, haven't you?'

'Aye, but not here, not now!'

Gary's heart was pounding like the timer on a bomb. He wiped his forehead with his handkerchief again and thrust it back in his jacket pocket on the bench.

'Well, girls,' Des called as they approached. 'This is an unexpected pleasure.'

'The pleasure's all yours,' said Zee sourly. 'I haven't seen you here before.'

'You come here often then?' asked Des. 'I'll have to do a spot more sunbathing. Who's that lot?' he added, nodding at the group in the distance.

'Just mates,' she said shortly.

'From school? Lots of little beauties, eh?'

'Nobody I'd want to introduce you to.'

'Hear that, Gary? Your sister wants to keep me all to herself.'

Gary ignored Des. He was watching Tasha who so far hadn't even looked at him. 'How you doing?' he asked her. 'I've been ringing you all week, Tash.'

'Have you?' Her voice was high and brittle. It made her sound even posher than usual.

'I left loads of messages on your ansaphone.'

'Miguel usually plays that back,' said Tasha. Her face had turned a dull red and she was trembling.

'What's wrong?' he pressed but she shrank away from his touch and even started to gulp back tears.

'Now see what you've done!' Zee scolded him like a nanny. She must have spotted the hanky in his pocket because the next moment she had whipped it out for Tasha. It was followed, a split second later, by the package.

Thwack! It hit the ground and Gary and Des drew breath sharply. Des even bounced back a step. Zee's eyes expanded like balloons.

'What is that?' she demanded, suspicion all over her face.

'Nothing!' They answered together and Gary whisked the parcel back into his jacket before anyone else could move.

'Nothing? Look at the pair of you – guilty as sin!' Zee's hand shot to her mouth in horror. 'Jesus! You're carrying packages for someone!'

'Shut up, will you?' hissed Gary, but luckily there was no one close enough to hear her.

'Are you mad? You could get yourselves killed!'

'It's not what you think,' lied Gary. 'It's ... CDs for a friend.'

'CDs?'

'Aye, honest.'

'Why would you wrap CDs up in brown paper? Why would you tape them up like that? Why would you meet someone here to hand them over?'

If Gary hadn't been so worried himself he would have lied more convincingly. He heard himself fumbling for words. 'The guy I'm giving them to works, so he does. This park's on his way home.'

'Prove it,' said Zee bluntly.

'What?'

'Open the parcel and show me the CDs.'

'Don't be soft! Sure I've only just wrapped them up.'

'Liar! Eejit! What'll Mum say? It'll kill Mum.'

'No, it won't,' said Des, catching her wrist. 'Because you won't tell her, will you?' Zee pulled hard but he held his grip. 'Be a good girl now and

105

promise me that you won't tell.'

'All right!'

He let her go slowly. Zee looked as if she might spit at Des but instead she spun round to face Gary. 'You don't know what you're getting yourself into!'

'It's all right, sis.' He hadn't called her that for years. Usually he treated her like something the cat had sicked up. 'I'll be careful,' he promised.

'How can you be? Dad told us – they just *start* by asking you to carry packages. Soon they'll be telling you to drive cars and hide guns. Then they'll want you to shoot the guns. Is that what you want, Gary? What you really want? Because those guys don't let people just up and leave them – Dad told us that too. You could end up in a ditch somewhere with a bullet in your knee at the least.'

Gary was torn. He didn't want to bottle out but Zee was only saying what he knew himself.

'Get outa here, girls,' growled Des. 'We've business to do.'

Out of the corner of his eye, Gary saw a BMW pull up at the park gates. Jimmy and Ben clambered out then stayed put, weighing up the scene. Zee looked over at the two heavyweights and it was enough to silence her.

'Go on,' said Gary. 'You'd best leave.'

Tasha had been looking on, bewildered, but now she turned to Zee. 'Lord knows what Gary and Des are up to but I'll bet my best earrings they're not going to listen to you!' She put her arm round Zee and started walking her towards an exit.

Gary stared after them. It was a long time since he'd seen Zee that upset, and as for Tasha, there was something irresistible about her.

'Will you pay attention?' Even Des sounded scared now.

Gary picked up the donkey jacket as the two men approached and every muscle in his body seemed to lock.

'They your girlfriends?' asked Jimmy.

'I wish,' said Des. 'That's Gary's sister and her mate.'

'Only they didn't look too happy – not interfering were they?' Jimmy was the less Neanderthal of the two but he still looked as if he could go a few rounds with an orang-utan, and he was after an explanation.

'Nah! She just wanted money,' said Des, adding, 'we didn't give her any, of course.'

Gary added, 'We just bumped into them.'

'Next time,' said Ben, staring hard at them, 'make sure you don't bump into anyone. Right?'

His voice reminded Gary of a snake slithering through frosty leaves. He wished more than ever that he had said no when Des came up with this crazy money-making scheme.

'Hand it over then,' said Des out of the corner of his mouth.

Gary glanced round quickly, then pulled out the package and slipped it to Ben.

The man's eyes flashed like missiles. 'Next time put it in a bag, dumbo.'

Gary nodded; his mouth seemed to have had dried up completely.

'Er – you said a ton...' muttered Des.

'Fifty.' Jimmy pulled out a wallet and peeled off five tenners. Even Des wasn't going to argue. 'Don't spend it all in one shop.'

'And...next time?' asked Des. 'You said, next time. When'll that be?'

Gary felt his stomach turn over. 'Forget it, Des.'

Ben's eyes glittered as he looked Gary up and down. 'Has golden boy here got a yellow streak up his back then?'

'Nah, just an honest streak,' Des said quickly. 'His da was a cop.'

'Was?'

'Aye, killed by the IRA.' Des sounded proud, his chest had practically puffed out. Anyone would have thought he was talking about his own father.

Ben looked at Gary with some sort of sinister approval. 'That so?' he said quietly. 'No surrender, right?'

Suddenly Gary felt sickened. Des could keep their filthy money; he wanted no part in this. These guys were thugs, plain and simple. His father would have locked them both up, and here was he, behaving just like them. A bit of Fenian baiting was one thing but getting involved with the likes of Jimmy and crazy Ben was something else entirely.

'What's in that package?' Gary asked quietly.

Silence went swirling around like poisoned gas. Des backed off and, for a moment, Gary thought his best mate was about to bolt.

'Does it matter what's in it?' asked Jimmy coolly.

'Mebbe.'

'Gary...' warned Des, 'leave it!'

Gary drew a deep breath. 'If it's explosives, yeah – it matters.'

Ben barked a bitter laugh. 'When was the last time you heard a bomb in Belfast?' he asked. 'More's the pity.'

'We've a right to know,' Gary pressed. 'We did the dangerous bit, we picked it up from that locker at the sports stadium. We carried it all the way here.'

'Doesn't he know the rules?' sparked Ben angrily.

'Shut up!' hissed Des. 'Have you totally lost it?'

But Gary couldn't stop. 'Or mebbe it's drugs? *Is it*?'

Ben's fist came up fast and exploded like a firework in Gary's stomach. For a moment Gary couldn't breathe at all. Doubling over, he saw the bulge of a big knife beneath Ben's shirt.

Des grabbed him and pulled him away backwards. 'Too much sun,' he told them apologetically. 'He doesn't mean it – sorry!'

Jimmy and Ben didn't speak, they just kept on staring.

'*I'm* still up for work,' mumbled Des. 'Trust me.'

Ben shook his head doubtfully. 'Don't hold your breath,' he said.

11

'By the bleeding hearts of the sacred saints of Ireland!'

Zee had been practising Catholic oaths for a whole fortnight now. She loved them, adored how the Papists swore in complete sentences; it made her body tingle with satisfaction in a way that muttering the odd clipped Protestant swearword never had.

At times like these, she thought, when a basket of multi-grain rolls had just nose-dived to the lawn, you really needed a good strong Fenian oath.

'What do you think, girls?' asked Magda, helping Zee pick out bits of grass and toss the rolls back into their wicker basket.

'It looks brilliant,' Zee told her. 'We haven't had a party in Hazel Grove for months – and not a garden party for years.'

'It's time we made an effort to meet the neighbours. I hope everyone enjoys themselves. Especially you, Tasha,' she added, 'you've not been yourself lately.'

'Oh, who have I been?'

Magda's nostrils flared in irritation but she stifled a reply and turned back to Zee. 'I'm particularly looking forward to meeting your mum.'

'Oh.' It came out as a squeak, like an animal in pain. Zee was dreading them meeting. How many times lately had she told her mum that she was going to see Tasha when really she was sneaking off to meet Conor? If that came out in the conversation she would be dead meat. Gary, Des and her mother would all queue up to murder her.

'Tasha says she's a keen gardener,' Magda went on.

'Mum can make just about anything grow.'

'Then I hope she'll give me some hints.' Magda groaned as she surveyed her garden. The newly cut lawn rolled away in front of them with all the character of an airstrip. The flowerbeds edging it were lumpy and bare.

'I'm sure she'd be happy to,' said Zee, making a mental note to encourage it; gardening was a safe topic. Conor was her main concern but another niggling worry was that her mum might cry. This garden party was a First and she nearly always cried at Firsts. The First Christmas without Dad, the First swimming trip, the First Sunday drive. Please God, prayed Zee, *please* don't let her cry.

'At least the twins will have fun stuffing themselves,' said Tasha, cutting into her thoughts.

'Those two could run riot here,' warned Zee, eyeing the white linen clad tables with a sense of doom. She could visualise pyramids of crockery crashing to the ground, a landslide of sandwiches, a waterfall of shattering glass...

'You leave them alone,' said Tasha, 'they're great!' Lately she had grown fond of Josh and Gemma who were still thrilled to find someone almost grown up who would happily spend time creating dinosaur lands with them or building dens. 'I wish I had a little brother or sister,' she added.

'Sorry,' said her mum. 'I'm a bit past all that.'

Magda looked stunning in a green silk dress which emphasised her perfect figure. Around her neck a string of glass beads glittered and her salon-shiny bob swung like a ship's bell. Zee hoped forlornly that her own mother would remember to change out of her holey gardening slacks before she came over.

'Come on,' said Magda, 'we need to help Miguel manoeuvre his piano to the French windows. I've persuaded him to play this afternoon.'

'Deep joy,' muttered Tasha.

'What is the matter with you?'

'I thought he might give it a rest today, that's all. I spend half my life listening to Miguel bashing away at that thing.'

'Whether you listen to him this afternoon is up to you,' said Magda curtly. 'But right now you'll help us move the piano.'

Later, when Magda had gone to check the sausage rolls in the oven, Zee quizzed Tasha. 'You are going to stick around this afternoon, aren't you?'

'Maybe.'

'Maybe? Like ... maybe *not* if Gary turns up?'

'Don't look at me like that, Zee. He's driving me mad. He won't stop phoning me. Sometimes he rings three times in one day. Even Miguel got fed up and yelled down the phone at him – but Gary's still ringing.'

'So why don't you talk to him? Explain that it's all over. I know Gary can be a pain, but he's got his pride – I bet he'd leave you in peace after that.'

112

'He's – he's kind of stuck on me.'

'You can't avoid him for ever, Tash.'

'No?' Tasha folded her arms defiantly. 'Just watch me,' she said.

The Munros from Number 16 arrived first. They talked about property prices until the Murrays from Number 22 arrived, then the two families exchanged prolonged comments about the unusually settled weather. Old Mr Cummings, another keen gardener, leaned on his stick and frowned at the empty flowerbeds. Then the O'Keefes came, en masse, all scrubbed up in their Sunday Best. Conor nodded hello to Zee then he ignored her as arranged.

When Johnny MacGuinness arrived with his wife, Connie, everyone relaxed. It was impossible to be straitlaced with Johnny around.

'Isn't MacGuiness a Catholic name?' Tasha asked Zee quietly. 'Those two seem awfully popular.'

'They're good fun – and they don't have any kids.'

'So?'

'So they're not a threat to Protestant Ulster,' said Zee wickedly, 'unlike the O'Keefes who have eight kids. Remember, when there's a majority in the North who want a united Ireland, we'll probably have one.'

'Is that why Catholics here have such big families?'

'We Prods do too! We take our responsibilities seriously, you know.' Zee grinned. 'Of course, Johnny MacGuiness provides an important public service too.'

'You told me he was a bookie.'

113

'Exactly.'

Johnny was wheezing with laughter as he told a story, his face as creased as a clown's.

'Worried?' he replied to a question. 'I wasn't a bit worried when I saw those scoundrels had pinched me Rover. They hadn't touched me ould Lada – the two cars were sitting there like Jack and Jill, side by side in me drive.'

'Surely you'd rather they'd taken the Lada than the Rover?' asked Mr Munro.

'The doors wide open in both of them,' laughed Johnny. 'Alarms off. But in the Lada there was five thousand pounds in the glove compartment!'

He folded up in laughter amid exclamations all round and he only just managed to wheeze out an explanation. 'An outsider came in last Thursday – Ice Cool at fifty to one. Sure, I made a packet out of Ballyrainey the favourite. I just hadn't got round to banking it – wouldn't the toe-rag of a thief be sick if he knew he'd driven away from five thousand quid!'

Zee was still laughing when Des's oily voice startled her.

'Hello, darlin'.'

He stared at her tanned shoulders, bare beneath the thin orange straps of her sun top. Out of the corner of her eye, Zee could see Conor watching from a distance. She took a step back but Des just lurched towards her. Picking up a tray of smoked salmon sandwiches she positioned it carefully in between them.

'Help yourself, Des,' she said.

'Fish pieces – yuck!'

He had the social graces of a pig, thought Zee. How could she ever have put herself in a compromising position with Desperate Des? When Gary appeared a moment later Zee almost felt relieved.

'Where's Tasha?' demanded Gary, a little out of breath.

'She was here a minute ago.' Zee looked around in surprise.

'I know that, I saw her.'

Des was leering again. 'I wish I had Tasha's powers of evaporation,' Zee muttered awkwardly.

'I need to talk to her.' Gary lowered his voice. 'You're her mate, Zee. What's wrong with her? Why won't she see me?'

'Lots of reasons. Maybe she doesn't like the friends you keep for starters.'

'You mean those guys in the park? I won't be doing any more jobs for them – I swear.'

'Good.' Zee scowled at Des. 'I was thinking of friends closer to home, actually.'

Des guffawed loudly, spluttering lemonade, or possibly something stronger. 'Gary and Tash had a great time together, Zee – know what I mean?'

'Stop shouting,' she hissed, 'you're making a show of us.' People were glancing round and – worse – Conor was moving closer. Zee felt panic bubbling up, like sweat on the inside. 'I've gotta go,' she told them.

'I'll go with you, darlin'.' Des flung his arm around her neck. 'We can find ourselves a wee quiet corner, somewhere. Take up where we left off. Whaddaye say?'

'No thanks!' Zee shook him off in disgust.

'Come on. Gimme a chance to change your mind.' His arm went round her shoulders again and this time it took a shove to get rid of him.

'I'm *not* going to change my mind, Des.'

'Aye you will. You're up for it.'

'What did you say?'

'All girls are up for it.'

Zee lost it. Was she to blame if Des was as thick as mince? Some people just needed to be told. 'All girls are *not* up for it,' she shouted at him, 'you got that? I wouldn't go with you if you were the last man on the planet. You look like you need plastic surgery, you've got a mouth like a megaphone, and if you'd more than one brain cell you'd be dangerous. Now once and for all *leave me alone*!'

Around them conversations stopped. Mrs Murray's mouth puckered up like a drawstring purse. Johnny MacGuinness looked fit to explode with laughter again, and she saw Des's mum turn her back. But worst of all Conor came shooting through the crowd like a missile, and landed right in front of Des.

'You heard her,' he said. 'Anything you didn't understand, Mastermind?'

Des swung for him. The punch didn't land because Conor just leaned back and Des whirled right round and fell over. It wasn't till then that Zee realised he was drunk.

'Conor,' she warned, 'this has *nothing* to do with you.'

Gary looked thoroughly pleased with her. He

practically swaggered as he leaned into Conor's face. 'That's you told, Fenian boy. Get lost!'

Conor scowled back at him. 'Are you sure you want me to leave you with these two, Zee?'

'Too right I am!'

He shot her an offended look and drifted off reluctantly. The other guests returned to their conversations. Des struggled to his feet.

'Why didn't you hit him, Gary?' he cried, dusting himself off.

'This is a party, Des, a posh do.'

'That Fenian insulted me!'

'Away and lie down, or get a drink or something.' Gary sounded fed up. 'I've gotta find Tasha.'

But Des was livid. Zee could tell that even if Gary couldn't. Des's plump face was twitching and he grabbed her arm.

'Why d'you show me up like that? I'll get you – bitch!'

'You? You couldn't get a suntan in a heatwave!' Something stopped Zee there. Something horrible about the way he looked at her. It was the same thing that had scared her back at the football pitch, a wildness just behind his face. As if there was something really nasty inside him, something tied down – but only just.

'There's Mum!' Spotting her with relief, Zee had spoken out loud.

'Better go to Mommy then!'

Zee darted through the crowd and Gary followed her, muttering about Zee being the one with a mouth like a

117

megaphone. Small children had started rolling down the grassy banks and the big lawn was busy. There was a hum about the place now and the sun was hot. Zee heard snippets of conversation about holidays and DIY and, of course, endless Irish politics. Her mother stood at the edge of it all, looking a little nervous with the twins pegged one on each side of her.

'Mum, you made it!'

'Of course I made it,' she replied. 'You make me sound like a nervous wreck.'

'What are you wearing?' asked Gary, walking right round his mother. 'Is that a curtain?'

'I told her she looked like the sofa,' chirped Josh.

Gary laughed rudely. 'You should have made yourself a matching hat – out of a cushion cover.'

Zee heard her mother's tone sharpen. 'Gary, have you been drinking?'

'Would I?' he said innocently but he melted away at once.

Gemma let out a whoop of delight. 'Look at those meringues, Josh!'

'Only one,' Zee told them sternly, 'and no playing under those tables. They might collapse and all that food would ruin. And don't try lifting one of those big Coke bottles – especially don't shake them – and see you mind your language!'

Whether they paid the slightest attention Zee couldn't tell but her stomach coiled up as she watched them depart for the food.

'So, where's Magda?' asked her mother. 'I really

ought to have made the effort to come and say hello before now.'

Zee led her towards a sycamore tree where Magda and Miguel were greeting neighbours. There was no escape now, thought Zee, no way she could postpone this meeting for a moment longer. 'You really should treat yourself to a new dress, Mum,' she agonised.

'I would if I had a bit more money.'

But Magda did not seem to notice the dress. 'Hello, Sue!' she cried as they approached. 'I've been longing to meet you. We think your daughter is wonderful, don't we, Miguel?'

'Thank you, Magda – I think she's pretty special too.'

'It's so nice that she and Tasha have made friends. Zee has promised me your gardening expertise, you know. I hope you don't mind?'

'You could lose out,' said Sue, twinkling.

'I thinks not. This garden – it is too big,' warned Miguel rolling his eyes heavenwards.

'I can see it's quite a challenge but I'd be delighted to give you advice.'

Zee felt proud of her mother. Magda might be a successful and hard-working juggler of home and career, but her mum had her very own charm. They talked rose bushes and rockeries and water features until Zee coughed meaningfully.

'Zee's quite right,' said her mother apologetically. 'I'm monopolising you. We'll talk again, Magda.'

'Help yourself to plonk and plenty food. We have much food.'

119

'Well done, Mum!' said Zee. 'You were great.'

Sue squeezed her arm. 'So I haven't lost my touch, then?'

'What touch?'

'Confidence. It happens to us stay at home mums, you know.'

'You don't *have* to stay at home,' Zee pointed out. 'The twins aren't babies any more and we're all more settled now – even Gary. You could go out to work if you wanted to.'

'I know.'

'And you could do with some new gear... we all could. You should see some of Tasha's stuff, it's beaut—' She broke off in dismay.

'It's okay, love, you've been very patient. I don't know how I'd have coped without you... and I'm not blind. I do know you'd love some new clothes. As a matter of fact, I've been thinking about work lately.'

'You never said.'

'That's because I'm still thinking. I wouldn't want any old job. It would have to be something interesting that I could fit around the family. Now, fancy a glass of wine?'

'Me?' Her mother was full of surprises today. 'Yes, please.'

'Just one, mind,' laughed Sue.

Zee relaxed as the fruity white wine went down. The introduction she had dreaded was over and there was no blood on the lawn after all. Her spirits lifted at the sight of Sue laughing and nattering with the neighbours. Not a tear threatened. Maybe things really were getting back to normal.

At the far side of the lawn a football game had got underway on a patch of rough grass and most of the neighbourhood kids were involved. She could see Conor and Josh both mid-field. Gemma sat on the sidelines tucking into a plate of sticky buns and Des was flaked out asleep.

On the patio in front of the French windows, Miguel was about to start playing the piano. Would Tasha really miss that? Zee scanned the crowd again but however carefully she looked there was no sign of Tasha or Gary. Surely Gary would not have slipped indoors uninvited?

Zee's stomach began to churn. Should she do something? What was going on? Where on earth were they?

12

Gary sneaked into the house and prowled along the tiled hall. He peered into the littered kitchen first, then the lounge. This had a stamp of Miguel about it. There was a gap by the French doors where his piano must surely stand, and beside it, tacked to the wall, was a photo-montage of dozens of heavily clad refugees fleeing some bombed out city. A huge map of south eastern Europe was pinned to another wall. Somehow Gary understood right away that Miguel needed to see that map every day.

'Tasha,' he whispered but there was no reply.

At the foot of the stairs he hesitated, one hand on the newel post. If they caught him upstairs they might get the police to him. Right then, a piano began tinkling outside as gently as a fountain. Everyone would be gathering around the patio now, all eyes on Miguel, everyone except Tasha and him. Impulsively Gary skimmed up the stairs.

'Tasha,' he called but again there was no answer.

He reckoned her parents would have the biggest bedroom. Parents always did unless there were tons of kids. That would be the room above the big lounge at the front. The small room above the dining room at the back of the house would probably be used for storage. That left three rooms, and the bathroom door was ajar which narrowed it down to two.

A low murmur drew him to a heavy oak door. What if it swung open? What if he disturbed a couple doing it? Nah! It wasn't that kind of party. Gary wiped the sweat off his face but he kept his weight on one leg, poised to spring back if he heard footsteps. The voice groaned on, low and monotonous, rising and dipping endlessly. Gary almost laughed aloud; it was a racing commentary.

He knocked, then knocked again, harder this time, and harder still until the dark wooden panel rattled beneath his fist. Whoever was in there must hear that, surely. No one answered and the commentary stayed at exactly the same pitch. Perhaps someone had gone outside and left the TV on. Perhaps the room was empty after all. Slowly, quietly, he turned the brass handle and peered round the edge of the door.

'Get out!' she screamed at him.

'Tasha!' She was standing by the window, one hand clutching the curtain. 'You *are* in here. Why didn't you answer me? You had me spooked.'

'*You* were spooked?' she gasped. 'What about me?'

He shut the door behind him and stared around her bedroom. 'Jeez . . . this all yours?'

'No, I share it with three hundred refugees – they're all hiding under the bed – what do you think, brain box?'

'I think you're lucky.' He closed the door behind him. 'Dead lucky.'

'Why don't you come in?' she cried, flinging away the curtain. 'Make yourself at home, Gary.'

'If you insist.' To cover up his awkwardness he squatted down and inspected her video. He checked out her sound system and ran a finger over the racks of CDs. Now he was here he didn't know what to say.

'Are you casing this house?' she asked suspiciously.

'That's not nice!' He feigned surprise. 'Me a cop's son too.'

'You? Your father was a policeman?'

'Yeah. Didn't Zee tell you that?'

Tasha shook her head, her blue eyes wide. 'She doesn't talk about him.'

'That's my sister for you.' Gary felt a chill creeping over him. 'Know what? I've seen the wee cow more upset over a dropped ice cream.'

He saw that he had shocked her now and he was more tongue-tied than ever.

'Why have you come up here?' she demanded shrilly.

'You didn't leave me any choice. Why are you shaking, Tasha? I'm not gonna hurt you! I just want to know what's going on. Why have you been avoiding me lately?'

'I haven't.'

'Not much! How come you're hiding up here when the rest of the street's partying?'

'Maybe I don't like parties.'

'Tasha... what is the problem?'

'You really don't know, do you?' He had never seen anyone actually wring their hands before but Tasha was doing it now. 'I don't want to see you again,' she said, 'so please, *please* leave me alone. All these phone calls... it's got to stop, Gary.'

'*Why* don't you want to see me? That's what I want to

know. We were all right together, you and me. How come you don't you want to see me suddenly?'

'I just don't.'

'Just don't? What kind of answer's that?' Gary could hear himself shouting. He wished he'd hadn't drunk any alcohol, then he might be able to think more clearly. 'You can't just walk off and leave me. There has to be a reason, Tash.'

'The reason is I didn't...enjoy...that night.'

He felt the colour shooting through his cheeks. For a moment he couldn't think of a word to say. 'I don't usually have complaints,' he quipped.

Then, to his horror, she let out a huge sob. He didn't have the first idea what to do. He tried to put his arm around her but she shrank angrily away.

'Don't touch me!'

'Why n—? What the hell's wrong?'

'You are! You didn't use a condom,' she shouted. 'Was I not even worth a condom, Gary?'

'Bloody hell, Tash...I thought you were on the pill.'

'You didn't ask, you didn't *even* ask me!'

Her words hit him like stones. 'Oh my God...are you...? Tasha, you're not...pregnant, are you?'

'Don't worry, *you're* all right.' She spat out the words as if he was dirt. 'I got the morning after pill – so no – I'm not pregnant!'

'Thank God.' Relief showered over him but his words didn't sound right, not even to him. 'Sorry,' he added quickly. 'Did...did you have to go alone to get the morning after pill?'

125

'No,' she snapped.

'Who went with you ...?' Mortified, he whispered, 'Not your ma, surely?'

'As if!'

'Who then?'

She turned bright red. 'Conor paid for a taxi.'

'Conor?' Gary ran his hand backward through his hair and tried to make sense of this. '*Conor*? You mean Con O'Keefe knows *our* business?' Humiliation raked him like gunfire. 'Why did that Fenian git go with you?'

'Stop shouting, Gary!'

She looked terrified and she had backed right up to the curtain again. Staring at her, Gary understood at last.

'You're going with *him*,' he declared. 'That's why you don't want me – you're going with Con O'Keefe!'

Her head bobbed up defiantly. 'So? What if I am?'

'I'll kill him!' swore Gary and he bolted from the room. 'I'll bloody murder him.'

'Leave him alone! You don't know what you're doing, Gary!'

Tasha rattled down the stairs behind him, pulling at his shirt. 'Leave him alone!'

He flicked her off like a wasp and yanked open the lounge door.

'Miguel!' cried Tasha and her voice had an edge like a power saw. 'Stop him, please stop him!'

Miguel was closing the French windows on a burst of applause and as he turned round to them he was smiling happily. 'So what is this? You have been where?' he asked.

'Please – he's going to kill Conor!'

'Oh?' Miguel looked sceptical but he stayed in front of the French windows, blocking Gary's way. 'Killing Conor would ruin the party,' he warned.

Gary took a deep breath. 'I'll take him somewhere else then.'

'And you are who, young man?'

'Gary,' said Tasha.

'Aaah. Gary of the great phone-bills?'

'It's all because I won't go out with him. He's jealous.'

'So, a crime of passion?'

Miguel was laughing at them. Gary felt like punching him right on his greasy nose. 'Your stepdaughter's seeing a Fenian,' he hissed, 'what do you think of that, eh? A Taig...Catholic scum!'

Miguel's good humour crumpled into a snarl and the next moment his hands fastened like mechanical grabs on Gary's shoulders. Gary felt himself being hoisted and shaken out like a dirty dishcloth.

'Catholic, Protestant, Christian, Muslim, what is the difference?' Miguel demanded. 'Must the whole world die before we have peace?'

Gary was five foot ten but Miguel pushed him through the house and propelled him out of the back door. 'You will not spoil this party. You will not upset Tasha. You will get off this property or I call the police.'

'Okay, okay!'

Gary spun backwards and fell over on the grass. When he had picked himself up he turned to Tasha, ignoring her mad Bosnian stepfather.

'I won't give up,' he warned. 'You'll see.'

13

Zee stared at Tasha in disbelief. 'Gary thinks what?' she demanded.

'Well, it wasn't my fault!' Tasha sounded like a guilty little kid and she blushed all the way from the bottom of her neck to the top of her forehead. 'Gary leapt to his own conclusions.'

'You mean you let him leap!'

They were sitting together on the riverbank, seeking refuge from the hot midday sun in the dappled shade of the wood.

'There was nothing I could do,' wailed Tasha.

'You could have told him the truth.'

'I did – sort of. That's what got me into trouble. I told Gary about having to go to the clinic and the moment he heard Conor's name he went ape.'

'Of course he did! Why on earth did you mention Conor?'

'Because I didn't want to mention *you*. I was trying to protect you, Zee.'

'You don't half get yourself in some muddles, Tasha. How can you be so naive?'

Zee jumped up and walked along the riverbank, hurling stones into the water. Just for a moment she wanted space. How could Tasha who had seemed so sophisticated, so worldly, have put her foot in it this badly?

'I'm so sorry,' Tasha said, coming up behind her, 'really I am, but you never know, maybe it's for the best.'

'How do you work that out?'

'Well, Gary will never guess it's *you* going out with Conor now and maybe he'll leave me alone too. It might make life easier for us both.'

'What about Conor?' cried Zee, rounding on her. 'Will Gary leave Conor alone too? It sounds as if he'd have killed him yesterday if Miguel hadn't stopped him.'

'Gary's a hot-head – he'll calm down.' Tasha's pretty pale eyes widened. 'I really don't understand why people here get so worked up about religion. It's silly. I thought there wasn't supposed to *be* fighting any more.'

Zee had a sudden urge to slap Tasha. 'At least *try* and understand. There may not be as many bullets flying around these days but you can't stop people remembering. How do you stop people hating each other if you can't stop them remembering?'

'Lord knows.' Tasha's eyebrows arched in bewilderment. 'But Zee... *we're* still friends... aren't we?'

'That depends,' she relied curtly.

'On...?'

'On you keeping your brain switched on in future.'

'I have said sorry!' Tasha flung one jeaned leg over the other and tossed her head crossly. 'What do you want me to do, lick your boots?'

Zee relented a little, perhaps she was being too hard. 'I'm just dreading telling Conor,' she said.

'Don't then.'

'Now that really would be irresponsible. Conor has a right to know if Gary's out to get him. Why don't you come to the beach barbie next weekend, Tasha? Then we could tell him together.'

'Er... no thanks.'

'But you've hardly been out since that night at the Co-op.'

Tasha shrugged. 'I haven't wanted to go out.'

'Well... maybe it would be better if I told Con alone.'

'Yeah... if there's anything else I can do though?'

Zee grinned at her. 'Well... you know you said I could borrow your red silk jacket sometime?'

The beach bonfire had burned low at last and the great pile of driftwood they had gathered together to feed it with had dwindled to almost nothing. In contrast, a pyramid of empty cans had grown like the Eiffel Tower. The birthday boy, Liam, was plucking hopefully at a cheap guitar and a crescent of folk still hugged the fire, singing an occasional lyric when one of his tunes became half recognisable. Conor, replete with sausages and cider, was lying fully stretched out on the sand, his dark head in Zee's lap. She curled her bare toes happily around sand that was the texture of soft brown sugar, its cool graininess as soothing as a massage.

'I like your friends,' she whispered to Conor.

'They like you too.'

She dropped her voice lower still. 'You know, I've never been alone with this many Catholics before.'

Conor barked with laughter and she thumped his

shoulder playfully. 'I just meant I never thought I'd feel this safe with them.'

'They're going to sacrifice you on that fire at midnight, did I not mention it?'

'It's just as well Tasha isn't here,' said Zee, 'or *I* might have sacrificed her.'

Conor's chocolatey eyes gleamed in a smile. 'Don't you worry about Gary, he's no big deal.'

'You're amazing – d'you know that?' Zee had told him on the bus about Tasha's gaffe. She thought he might have slagged Tasha off, or even got paranoid, but no, Conor had just shrugged. Perhaps they were both right and she had over-reacted after all. Still, Zee couldn't imagine many blokes taking Gary's threats lightly. That made Conor special. That and his soft brown eyes. She bent down and kissed him on the lips. His eyes pulled her in like magnets, and she lingered there, kissing him gently.

'Fancy a walk?' he asked hoarsely.

She got up, shaking the sand out of Tasha's silk jacket and they wandered along the curve of silvered sand with the skelf of a new moon high above and waves frothing up the beach. Conor put his arm around her shoulders and she held his waist.

'Tide's coming in,' he murmured.

'Tides always seems so pointless to me, Con, those big waves pounding up the shore then going back out to sea. Doing nothing, going nowhere – and using all that energy to do it. I'd hate to be a wave.'

He laughed. 'You crease me up, Zee Proctor, do you know that?'

'Why?'

'You're always so busy working everything out, so . . . purposeful.'

Zee sighed. She had been hoping for something a bit more romantic than 'purposeful'.

It might have been the sigh but she liked to think it was telepathy that made Conor stop just then. He put his arms around her and in the moonlight they became one of several couples entwined along the sands at Helen's Bay.

They might have kissed for two minutes or for ten, Zee didn't know. Conor stroked her face, held her head tenderly between his hands, raked his fingers lovingly through her hair.

'Trust me,' he murmured and he took her hand. They crossed the beach to the sand-dunes where tall marram grass provided shelter and he pulled her gently down beside him. 'Okay?'

'Okay.' She let him unbutton her blouse and nuzzle between her breasts. She let him unhook her bra.

'You've got fantastic nipples,' he murmured.

'Have you – um – seen a lot of nipples then?'

He shook his head and ran his finger in little circles around her breast. With his tongue he licked the dark aureola until she trembled, then he sucked her nipple softly. It made her whole body tingle, every nerve seemed to come alive, electrifying her until she felt she must be sparkling like a chandelier.

Her heart was banging but not with fear this time. It was something much more complicated than fear. She fumbled clumsily with Conor's shirt, ran her hands up and down his back, filled them with his warm, firm flesh, gulped in the soft saltiness of his skin.

It was amazing but somehow her own senses had suddenly come alive. How could touch and smell have stayed hidden for so long, how could Conor waken so suddenly these feelings...this lust?

When she felt his hand in her jeans she slipped her own hand inside his and nervously, carefully, explored. She'd heard it called all sorts of names before. Dick, cock, prick. Vulgar names that never hinted at any intimacy and never ever suggested love.

'Okay?' he whispered again.

She nodded because she didn't trust her voice.

'The things they teach in these Protestant schools,' he teased. They lay there, holding each other and kissing tenderly as waves thumped up the beach and the stars shone down.

'Zee,' he murmured, 'I've got a condom in my pocket.'

Her heart missed a beat. She felt, suddenly, out of her depth, so she played for time. 'Where did you get that?' she asked him.

'Someone gave the birthday boy dozens.'

'So he shared them out? Very egalitarian...very laddish.'

She heard him hesitate. 'Well, Zee?'

'I...do you mind if we don't...not yet?'

Conor groaned and rolled away from her. It felt as if an iron door had come rattling down between them.

'I really am sorry,' she whispered.

'Then why not...?'

'I'm not ready, not yet. Can you understand?'

'Yeah.' A moment later he rolled back to her. 'Actually, no, I don't understand at all. I know we're supposed to, us blokes, but I don't. I thought you were enjoying it.'

'I was. That doesn't mean I want to go all the way.'

'That's the bit I don't understand. *Why* don't you?'

Zee groped for an explanation. How could she explain it? She hardly understood herself. 'It's different for girls,' she said lamely.

'How?'

'Sex is just an adventure for guys, Con.'

'No it isn't!' His forehead dived into a frown. 'Well...maybe it is, but so what?'

'It's different for us. It's a really big deal. You go inside us, sort of...take us over.'

'Take you over?' His face brightened. 'You could go on top, I wouldn't mind.'

'That's not the point! You go *inside* us – like an invasion – it's risky for us...don't you see?'

'I'm trying to...'

'It's just the way we're made – different. It means girls have got to be really dead sure they want to.'

'I thought you were sure, Zee.'

'About you...I am. But not about the physical stuff – not yet. Anyway, there's more between us than that, isn't there?'

'You know there is,' he said.

'Then wait till I'm ready.' She kissed him again.

'Tonight's been brilliant for me, you know.'

Conor cleared his throat. 'Any idea...when you... might want to?'

'No,' she laughed. 'But you'll be the first to hear when I do.'

'I should hope so.'

'And Con...I can't be worrying every time we go for a walk together. Know what I'm saying?'

'No pressure, right?' He sighed heavily. 'You're a hard woman, Zee.'

'Come on, we'd better not miss the last bus.'

He grabbed her hand, keeping her there for a moment longer. 'One more thing,' he said.

'What's that?'

He put his arms around her one more time. 'Zara Proctor,' he said, 'I love you.'

The party continued on the bus. Noisy groups were clustered on the top deck determined to enjoy every last minute of their Saturday night. They sang and shouted good naturedly and passed around cans of beer, making bawdy comments to groups of girls who flirted back. A ghetto blaster drowned out most of the conversation and four people shared a messy Chinese meal, rice flying off their plastic forks at every bend in the road. Zee would have been scared if she had been there with Tasha, game for every bloke on the bus. But safe with Conor, she felt fine.

At Hazel Grove they got off and walked the short distance home. The perfume of roses, sharper somehow in the darkness, floated up from the neat front gardens. Only a few lights were still on.

'They'll all be up by nine o'clock,' moaned Zee, 'in church by eleven and lunch at one. Then they'll spend the afternoon washing their cars. It's all so predictable round here – sometimes I want to explode!'

Conor laughed at her. 'Most folk like a bit of routine, you know.'

'Not me. A trip to the supermarket the highlight of the week? No thanks.'

Just then they came over the hill, within sight of the O'Keefes' house and they both stopped dead.

'No!' Panic fizzed through Zee's stomach, waves of it radiating out until her arms and legs were trembling too. She remembered that feeling, that awful, uncontrollable shaking. It had happened to her once before; the night they killed her father.

'My God!' said Conor. 'Is that unpredictable enough for you?' But he was shocked too. He pulled her into the shadows and held her until her tremors stopped.

'It's Gary's work,' she whispered. 'What's he thinking of?'

Conor gave her a gentle push. 'Go home,' he whispered. 'Go by Tasha's in case anyone's watching.'

'What will *you* do?' she choked.

'Conor!' shouted an urgent voice. 'Get you in here!' It was his father calling and all their lights were switched off.

'Not much I can do,' Con said bitterly. 'I'll have to go in. Will you be all right?'

136

'It's *you* I'm worried about.'

Zee pulled the collar of Tasha's jacket up around her ears and walked quickly on. Someone was watching her, she could feel it. Feel their eyes, hard as nails, hammering into her back.

She couldn't help looking up. Impulsively, unable to stop herself, she glanced in at the Gordons. Upstairs, the bathroom curtain slid back into place. But not before she had seen the pale glimmer of Des's face staring down at her. Zee gasped and hurried towards Tasha's. If she had seen Des Gordon, then Des had certainly seen her.

The graffiti was everywhere; red like blood, a spray can judging by the edges, all over the garden wall and on the footpath outside too.

FENIANS OUT!

CON O'KEEFE YOU HAVE BEEN WARNED.

GET OUT OR BE BURNED OUT.

ULSTER

IS OURS.

14

Conor's front door edged open just a few inches and his father yanked him inside.

'Just what the hell's been going on, Conor? What have you been up to?'

'Me? Nothing!'

Kevin O'Keefe was a small man but his rages were huge. Right now his eyes were bulging and his top lip was filmed with sweat. Behind him the entire family was massed on the stairs, like spectators at a football match.

'It's that wee English girl, isn't it? You've been messing around with her! Don't deny it – she was here the other week and I've just seen the pair of you outside with me own eyes.'

Conor didn't deny it. His glance swept over the entire family. He could only pray that Tasha's red jacket had duped them all. 'So? What if I have been seeing her?' he asked.

His father looked fit to burst. 'It's caused that mess outside, that's what!'

Conor jabbed his finger towards the graffiti. '*I* am not responsible for that!' he said and strode off down the hall.

'Come you back here! I'm talking to you! Don't you dare turn your back on me, boy!'

Conor filled a glass with cold water and gulped it

down. Sometimes he hated being the oldest son and he needed a moment to get his head straight. His father stormed into the kitchen behind him and snapped off the light.

'Don't make a target of yourself, y'eejit!'

'Aye, that's right, let's live like rabbits down a hole – scared to pop up our heads in case we get shot!'

'And who's to blame for that?'

Conor heard his mother shooing the rest of the family back to their beds. She closed the kitchen door quietly and pulled the tweedy curtains tight, then she switched on the spotlights above the worktop.

'Come on, now,' she said softly, 'you do owe us an explanation, Conor. We've never had any trouble here before. This isn't really about religion, is it? Is it that wee English girl, right enough? Is Gary jealous?'

Conor sipped thoughtfully at his water. 'Are you absolutely sure it was Gary?' he asked them.

'Him and some others,' said his father angrily. 'They were all wearing balaclavas but we heard Gary's voice all right. It was him giving the orders.'

'I'm surprised you and me brothers didn't go out to them.'

'I wanted to!' Kevin O'Keefe smacked his fist against the palm of his other hand. 'Your mam here wouldn't let me out the front door.'

'Do you blame me? Paint's one thing, Kevin, blood's another.' She turned back to Conor. 'We'll help you, son, whatever kind of trouble you're in – but you've got to be straight with us. You don't seem too surprised by all this.' Suddenly she was suspicious. 'Is there more? What's been going on?'

Conor took a deep breath and walked uncertainly to the back door. He dug into the pocket of his old wax jacket hanging on the peg and pulled out a crumpled envelope. It was a jacket he only wore for fetching coal in the rain. The note, tucked in an inside pocket might have stayed hidden there for years.

'It's only brief,' he mumbled, smoothing out the page inside.

They didn't say a word, they just stared at him, but he could feel how frightened they were. To his annoyance, his own hand trembled a little as he showed them the threat, an ugly red inked scrawl.

HANDS OFF

YOU ARE BEING WATCHED

WE LIVE BY THE GUN

'Holy God!' exclaimed his mother and her hands flew to her throat. His father's face blanched like an almond.

'When did that come?' he demanded.

'A couple of days ago.'

'And you went out tonight? Are you mad? Why didn't you tell us, Conor?'

'Because I knew how you'd react! I didn't want to worry everyone. It's only Gary Proctor.'

'Worry!' His mother laughed hysterically.

'It's not serious, Mam. He's only just stirring things up.'

'Is that really all there is to this ... jealousy?'

Conor couldn't look her in the eyes. 'Tasha doesn't feel the same way about him,' he mumbled, by way of explanation. 'She doesn't want to go out with him. Don't worry, he'll get over it.'

'All this over some silly wee girl?' exclaimed his father. 'Graffiti in Hazel Grove ... the shame of it ... what will the neighbours think?'

Conor slammed a cupboard door shut with his foot. 'Is that all you're worried about, Dad? The neighbours? God, parents can really let you down sometimes!'

'Don't you cheek me, Conor. Can't you see how embarrassing this is for us?'

'Ssh, Kevin,' urged his mother. 'Don't worry about the neighbours. They'll be as upset as us. We've friends in Hazel Grove, not just neighbours.'

'Friends?' Conor's father laughed bitterly. 'Where were these friends tonight, Maree, tell me that?'

Tears hung like polished beads in his mother's eyes and that got to Conor more than anything his dad might say. 'It'll be all right,' he muttered, putting an arm around her.

'Will it?' She shook her head. 'Poor Sue will be mortified. To think her wee Gary would grow up like this ... '

'Don't you start feeling sorry for Gary,' spluttered his father. 'That boy needs locking up.'

'But he's been through so much, Kevin. He saw his father killed, remember. His own father shot to bits all over the living room walls. Can you imagine? How can any child grow up normal after that?'

'Never mind him. God help *us* if he's got a bone to pick with our Con. First a letter, then graffiti. What will he do next, Maree? A beating? A knee-capping, what?'

For a fleeting moment Conor had a vision of the house in flames, kids screaming, knotted sheets hanging from the windows. After all, no one, not the politicians, not even the police could stop loonies with grudges. 'I'll get rid of the graffiti tomorrow,' he promised them.

'And I'll speak to Sue,' said his mother. 'We can't let this go any further.'

'No, Mam, you'll only make things worse.'

'Then you give that wee girl up,' said his father fiercely. 'Leave her to Gary. There's plenty nice Catholic girls around.'

Conor blushed with fury. Stick to your own kind... his own father was as sectarian as any of them. He couldn't trust himself to answer. What would he say anyway? How could he admit that it wasn't Gary's girl he was seeing, but Gary's sister? He wasn't sure who would go craziest, Gary or his own parents. Besides, he had absolutely no intention of giving up Zee.

'There is one other way,' said his mother quietly. 'You could take a holiday, son. Go to your Auntie Mary in Donegal. You'd be safe there. You might even find a job.'

'Doing what? Digging peat? Cleaning toilets for the tourists? You must be joking, Mam.'

'But you'd be safe!'

'I'm *not* running away.'

'Then you'd better come up with some other ideas,' said his father, 'pretty damned fast.'

Conor scowled at the pair of them. 'Give me a bit of peace,' he said, 'and maybe I will.'

Long after the house had settled down, Conor was still tossing ideas around in his head. What was the point in trying to convince Gary that he wasn't seeing Tasha? Gary wouldn't believe him. And if he did, it would probably only lead to something worse.

He remembered the marks Gary had left on Zee's shoulders on the twelfth of July. What would he do to her now if he found out the truth? Just how bitter and screwed up was Gary? Just how violent?

Conor thumped his pillow in frustration and little Diarmaid, in the nearest bed, groaned and turned over. Was Gary asleep, Conor wondered, or was he still trying to get red paint off his hands?

Would Gary really leave it at this? A letter and a bit of graffiti? What would happen next? What could he do to stop him?

Suddenly the answer hit Conor.

If Gary Proctor wanted satisfaction, let him have it. The two of them could sort things out right now. A few thumps and it would all be over. Even if Gary won, the idea of punching him was totally irresistible. Quietly, almost noiselessly, Conor swung his legs over the edge of the bed and felt for his clothes.

The Proctors' house was in darkness when he got

there but he knew exactly which was Gary's bedroom. They had played there together when they were kids, before they drifted apart, before he went to St Joseph's School and Gary to the nearest Protestant Primary.

Conor scooped up a handful of gravel and tossed it at the open window. There was no response so he picked up more stones and threw them up, one by one, until the curtain moved.

'Get down here,' he called softly.

'O'Keefe?' Gary sounded surprised, but almost pleased. 'What do you want?'

'Guess. Don't tell me I have to come up there and get you?'

The curtain dropped back. Moments later, Gary appeared on the steps at the back door, wearing only jeans and trainers. He flicked on an outside light, illuminating the lush summer garden. A black cat in the elephant grass watched them for a moment then leapt up a tree out of the way.

'Have you any idea how much trouble you've caused tonight?' Conor asked tersely.

'So your folks have taken the hint then?' said Gary, pleased. 'You're leaving?'

'In your dreams.'

'We don't want your kind round here, O'Keefe.'

'We? Who's that then? You and Desperate Des? Wake up, Gary, this isn't about religion.'

'Isn't it?'

'This is between you and me, right?'

Gary's face hardened. 'Tasha's *my* girlfriend.'

'Yours? What did you ever give her – besides one behind the Co-op?'

'You bast—'

'Cowboy without a condom,' interrupted Conor, 'that's what she calls you. As for your performance that night... one out of ten, she said.'

Gary flew off the top step and Conor felt as if he'd been hit by a juggernaut. Even though he'd expected it, provoked it, Gary's sheer power winded him. Somehow he managed to roll out of his grasp and pick himself up.

Gary lunged again and Conor gasped. He felt his cheek swell as fast as bubble gum, then he let fly himself, swinging his fists hard and fast until they connected with something. He had the satisfaction of seeing Gary Proctor double over. It was only for a moment though, then he found himself flying through the air and he hit the fountain. He felt a cold jet of water in his eyes and his head bounced down the stone figure. He couldn't get back up because Gary had climbed into the pond and his fists were firing into his back like bullets. Conor hedge-hogged and waited for Gary to exhaust himself.

'Stop this!' yelled a voice. 'Stop it! Stop it!'

'I'll kill him!' shouted Gary and Conor grunted as a kick sank into his kidney.

'No! Stop it!' shouted someone else.

It was a few moments before the blows stopped. When Conor looked up he saw three females holding Gary back and his own mother was one of them.

'Look at your fountain, Mum!' cried Zee. 'Your new fountain all broken and ruined.'

'Never mind the fountain,' cried Sue. 'What's going on here?'

'Are you all right, Conor?' His mother touched his cheek anxiously.

'Of course I am! What are *you* doing here? Why did you interfere, Mam?'

'You wee fool! Gary could have *killed* you.'

'We were sorting things out – finishing it.'

'What things?' demanded Sue, swinging from one boy to the other. 'Finishing what? Gary – answer me!'

But there was dead silence. It was Conor's mother who broke it eventually and she sounded almost apologetic. 'I'm afraid your Gary and his friends wrote graffiti on our garden wall tonight, Sue.'

'*What*?' Sue stared at her big son in disbelief. 'No...how could you, Gary? How could you do that?'

'He pinched my girl,' said Gary sullenly.

'Come again?' Sue started pummelling her fists against his chest. 'Your *girl*? What sort of a reason's that?'

'Stop it, Mum!' There was no chance she could hurt him but she kept going until he caught her hands in his own and held them still.

'What did you write?' she demanded. 'What did it say?'

There was another silence.

'Get out or be burned out,' supplied Conor, 'wasn't that it? Yeah, and that old gem – Ulster is Ours.'

Zee made a noise that seemed to catch in her throat. 'You still shouldn't have come down here!' she shouted. Conor shot her a burning look, willing her not to say too much.

146

'Your father,' Sue croaked angrily, 'will be turning in his grave with shame.'

Emotion raced across Gary's face, they all saw it; anger, guilt, hate. 'My dad would understand,' he yelled back. 'If it hadn't been for the likes of them, my dad would still be here!'

'Your father's death was nothing to do with us,' said Maree O'Keefe quickly. 'You *know* that.'

'He was killed by Catholics, wasn't he?'

'But not by *us*. Are you going to hate all Catholics for ever?' she asked.

'Why shouldn't I?'

Sue broke away, sobbing, and Conor's mother put her arms around her. 'We'll go on home now,' she said, 'and leave you in peace. I'm sorry my boy came down here tonight, Sue. Thank God he woke Diarmaid up, getting dressed, otherwise I'd never have known.'

Anger flared up in Conor again. Why could his mother not keep her nose out? 'This could have finished it,' he mumbled.

'Finished you more like,' mocked Gary. 'Take a look in the mirror, O'Keefe. Your ma just saved your pathetic little life!'

Sue Proctor drew herself up to her full height which was about six inches shorter than her son. 'I am so sorry, Maree,' she said. 'So very sorry, and tomorrow, first thing, Gary will paint out all that graffiti.'

'I will not.'

'Yes, you will.' Sue caught her breath and spoke very deliberately. 'Because if you don't, Gary, *I* will ring the police and tell them to charge you with criminal damage.'

Sue and Gary stood eyeballing each other for a full minute. It was only when Zee let out a sob that they turned around. She had sunk down onto the doorstep as if it was all just too much and tears were trailing down her face.

15

It was a long night. Zee lay with her eyes wide open, listening to her mother and Gary arguing in the kitchen. Gemma, woken by the noise, crept sleepily into bed beside her and curled her thin arms around Zee's neck. Eventually the arguing stopped, the lights went out, and Gemma's breathing slowed and deepened. But still Zee lay awake.

If only she hadn't fallen for Conor, none of this would have happened. Why had she asked Conor for the taxi fare that day? Why had she not gone to Melanie or Tracy or Pip?

Deep down Zee knew the answer and guilt scorched over her. No other boy had a smile that made her heart race, and when Conor's eyes softened and his voice dropped to a whisper, he made her ache with longing.

Perhaps she should tell Gary the truth now, before Des did. Perhaps it was not too late. It might stop him cracking up over Tasha, ruining the whole neighbourhood, murdering Conor. But what on earth would he do to her?

Next morning Zee woke with an aching head, but during the night one idea had taken shape. She must stop seeing Conor, just for a while, until people calmed down. Gary would be watching every move Conor made. Judging by the slamming of pots and pans downstairs, her mother was still furious too.

Zee sneaked the cordless phone up to her bedroom, dialled 141 and then rang Conor's number.

'Yes?' Mr O'Keefe's voice was gruff.

'Can I – er – speak to Con?'

'No,' he bawled and hung up.

The miserable old git. Zee threw down the phone in despair. How was she going to get a message to Conor now?

She wandered outside to where the twins were wisely keeping out of their mother's way. They had heard about the fight and they were busy picking stones and bits of grass out of the little pond.

Slowly, snail-like with tiredness, Zee climbed the laburnum tree. She separated the foliage discreetly, craned her neck, and sighed. There was Gary, guilty for the whole world to see, turping out his handiwork from the night before. And right beside him stood Ruby and Des. Zee couldn't help wondering just what Gary had ever done to deserve such loyalty.

Ruby had a cigarette in one hand and with the other she was thrashing a scrubbing-brush back and forth so violently that drops of red flew off it in all directions. She didn't look chuffed. Des was not actually working but his body language would have turned back a rattle-snake, let alone the mild-mannered residents of Hazel Grove. Neighbours hurried past, their heads down, on the way to church. They didn't say a word but Zee knew that her family would be the hottest gossip in the pews.

'*I* want to look,' demanded Gemma from ten feet below.

'Okay, but don't let Gary see you – he's not exactly in a good mood.'

'Neither's Mum,' moaned Josh, scowling up at her. 'She won't even take us to the shop for a lolly.'

'She can't face the neighbours, stupid,' said Gemma.

Zee felt a new pang of guilt. 'I'll take you later,' she promised, climbing down. 'I'll buy you both choc ices but I've got to see Tasha first.'

A new plan had formed in her head and she made for Tasha's, studiously ignoring Gary and his friends. Des spotted her at once though, and bellowed down the street.

'Well, well, look who it is!'

Zee hurried on but he shouted again and this time his voice was accusing.

'So what were *you* up to last night, Zee?'

With a jolt like an electric shock she saw triumph gleaming in Des's face. She said nothing but burst into a run, bounced across Tasha's gravel drive and leapt the three porch steps together.

'Des knows!' she cried as soon as the door opened. 'He knows about me and Conor. I'm sure he does!'

'Ssh!' Tasha's finger flew to her lips. 'He can't do, silly. He'd have told Gary and you'd be dead by now.'

It wasn't exactly reassuring. 'You've gotta help me,' begged Zee. 'You've got to take a message to Conor.'

'Me ... ?' Tasha backed off a step at the mere suggestion.

'You're not going to *believe* what happened last night.'

Magda, appearing from the kitchen, caught the last sentence. 'Puppy love?' she asked, grinning.

151

'No!' declared both girls at once.

She laughed. 'Before you vanish upstairs I've got something exciting to tell you. Twenty Bosnian refugees are going to be settled here next month.'

'Riveting,' said Tasha.

Magda ignored the sarcasm and continued enthusiastically. 'So ... two weeks on Saturday we're entertaining some local business people who are going to help fund the programme.'

'God, not a musical evening, Mum!'

'No, a dinner party. I'd like you to be there, Tasha.'

'What on earth for?'

'Because you're my daughter. Could you make it too, Zee?'

'Er – I think I'm busy that night.'

'Shame. You can help me choose menus, Tasha, and help with the cooking if you like.'

'Could we make Death by Chocolate for dessert?'

'Er – perfect.' Magda brushed her arm affectionately. 'I thought it might be fun to do something like this – you and me together.'

'Maybe.'

Tasha was not exactly bowled over with enthusiasm but Zee could tell that she was a little bit pleased. They went upstairs to her bedroom where Zee filled her in on the previous night's events. Afterwards, Tasha was even less keen to act as messenger.

'They're still out there,' she said, peering through the window. 'Gary and Des and that awful Ruby! I can't walk past all of *them*.'

152

'You owe me,' said Zee bluntly.

'Couldn't it wait till they've gone?'

'No. Heaven knows what Conor might do next. Or Gary. I tried ringing Con earlier but his dad hung up.'

'If only he had his own mobile...' Tasha stroked her polished nails rather rapidly. 'I *do* *want* to help, Zee... it's just that I'm not...er...awfully good at this sort of thing.'

'Don't try and worm your way out of it, Tasha.'

'Zee!'

'You got me into this mess – the least you can do is help me out of it. If you hadn't lied to Gary about going out with Conor, none of this would have happened. Not the graffiti, not the fight, nothing!'

'I know.' Tasha looked up at her miserably. 'I really am sorry.'

'Then take my message to him. He's got to understand that we can't risk meeting.'

Tasha swallowed hard. 'What if they attack me?'

'Gary's nuts about you, Tasha, he won't hurt you.'

'And Des?'

'It'll just confuse Des. If he sees *you* going in there it might put paid to his suspicions about *me*.' Tears sprang unexpectedly to Zee's eyes. 'Everything's got so out of hand, Tasha – we've got to stop it.'

'Oh, don't cry!' Tasha put an arm around her awkwardly. 'Okay...I will go...even if wild, witchy woman is out there.'

'Ruby? Does Ruby still bother you? I thought you didn't fancy Gary any more.'

Tasha pouted. 'That doesn't mean I want him fancying Ruby.' She took several deep breaths. 'Okay... scary people here I come.'

Tasha couldn't help feeling flattered by Gary's reaction as she made her way up the hill. Flattered and frightened. The look on his face as she stopped outside the O'Keefes' was as plain as banner headlines in the *Sun*. Even with Ruby's restraining hand on his arm, Gary looked as if he wanted to burst out of his own skin.

'Where are you going?' he cried as she turned towards the O'Keefes' gate.

'To talk to Conor,' she said shakily.

'Don't do that!'

'Leave her be,' muttered Ruby. 'Ye can't stop her ye know.'

Tasha gave Ruby a grateful nod and walked on self-consciously. Des was frowning nastily at her. He knew Zee's secret all right and his stare seemed to pin her to the pavement like a butterfly to a board. Tasha wished she was brave, like Zee, but inside, she felt hopelessly feeble.

'How ye doing?' Ruby went on, friendly enough. 'Ye okay?'

Tasha nodded again, struggled to find her voice, and waved her hand at the paint. 'This looks ghastly,' she managed at last.

Ruby sniffed disapprovingly. 'Aye, boys will be boys.'

Suddenly Des planted himself right in front of Tasha and she recoiled as if someone had thrown an adder under her feet.

'Can you remember what this said last night, Tasha?

Bet you can't!' His eyes narrowed suspiciously. 'What exactly are you up to?'

'Leave me alone, Des Gordon!'

'Yeah, leave her be,' said Gary. 'Quit messin'.'

'Ye jerk!' added Ruby. 'Let her past.'

Des stood aside reluctantly and Tasha flew past the metal gate in the wall, banging it shut behind her.

'Please don't go in there,' called Gary. 'You don't know what you're doing to me, Tash!'

Tasha wasn't enjoying the experience either. She hurried up the garden path and behind her she could hear Ruby trying to calm Gary down. She pressed the door-bell twice in quick succession and Conor hauled her inside.

'What the hell are you doing here?' he demanded.

'That's charming! I risked my neck coming to see you.'

'*Your* neck?' he said through clenched teeth. 'Have you any idea of the trouble you've caused?'

'Yes!' Recovering a little, she added, 'But you're not completely innocent yourself. It was *you* who picked the fight last night.'

He glared at her with his black eye, then said, 'So why have you come?'

'Zee begged me to, that's why. She's worried about you. Is...um...that eye painful?'

'It's fine. Sure I love looking like a liquorice allsort.' He thrust his face forward for a close-up of the ugly purple-black bruises and the livid red wounds. 'Meathead! If you hadn't told Gary we were going out, none of this would have happened.'

155

'I know.' Tasha bit her quivering lip. It was bad enough being a meathead. She didn't want to be a crybaby too. 'I've brought you a message, Conor.'

'What message?'

'Zee thinks that you shouldn't see each other for a while.'

'Great!' He banged the flat of his hand against his head. 'I knew this was coming, I just *knew* it.'

'Only for a while,' she repeated, 'until everyone calms down. Zee's terrified that Gary might do something else.'

'I wasn't planning to go outside and sunbathe.'

'She's scared for herself too. She saw Des at his window last night. She thinks he recognised her.'

Conor's eyes closed momentarily, then he started pacing up and down the hall. She could see that he was worried about Zee's safety even if he didn't care much about his own.

'And what do you think?' he asked, turning to her. 'Do you think Des knows?'

'He was . . . er . . . asking some funny questions just now.'

'And how did the Brain of Britain cope with that?'

'I did my best!' Tasha knew that she didn't impress Conor one little bit, he zoomed in on all her weak spots. 'There's no need to treat me like something that's stuck to your shoe,' she added. 'And yes, I think Des does know.'

Conor kicked the wall in frustration. 'It doesn't look like we've much choice, does it? My parents aren't going to let me out of their sight anyway. Okay, tell Zee we'll play it safe and stay apart for a while.'

156

Tasha sighed in relief. Perhaps it had been worthwhile coming after all. 'Zee said she'd meet you two weeks on Saturday – the day your exam results come out.'

'The fifth of August. Tell her to meet me well away from Hazel Grove – tell her to be at Bookbinder's at seven o'clock. And tell her—'

'Yes?'

He blushed. 'Never mind, she already knows. Now you'd better get outa here before my old man gets back from chapel and does something very unchristian to you.' He opened the front door again.

'Conor...I'm...I'm sorry. I had no idea all this would happen. It's mad over here!'

He glanced over her head to the gate. 'Maybe we should try harder to confuse Des. That shouldn't be difficult.'

'How? What do you mean?'

He took a deep breath. 'I promise, this is going to hurt me a lot more than it hurts you.' With that he put his arms around her, fastened his lips on hers and gave her a long lingering kiss. Tasha was so gobsmacked she almost fell over.

Gary started yelping like a foxhound. If Des and Ruby had not held him back, Tasha felt quite sure he would have torn Conor to pieces.

'I'll have you, O'Keefe,' he was yelling. 'You wait!'

Tasha fled out of the gate past the three of them and ran down the hill. Ruby was hushing Gary but it didn't stop him shouting after her.

'What are you doing to me, girl? You're doing my

157

head in! Tasha, you're crackin' me up!'

But somehow it wasn't Gary who frightened her. It was Des with his long penetrating stare that followed Tasha all the way home.

16

Des saw his mother come out of their house and frown over the hedge at the rumpus. He gave her a full hundred-watt scowl and she scuttled back indoors without a word. He wished Ruby would push off too. Gary was a lot easier to handle without her around.

'Calm down, Gary!' she was saying, 'Just listen to me. If anythin' happens to Conor now, ye'll be the one that gets the blame.'

'I say Gary's right,' Des told her. 'I think we should teach O'Keefe some manners.'

Ruby practically swallowed him whole. 'Who asked ye to say anythin'? Ye big eejit! You're more like seven than seventeen. Ye've not got the sense ye were born with.'

Des felt like slapping the backstreet tart but he managed to keep his hands by his sides. He turned to Gary. 'You just gonna leave it there? O'Keefe's got your girl, he's got the whole street giving you the cold shoulder and now he's standing on his doorstep winding you up!'

'Ignore Des,' snorted Ruby.

'O'Keefe's making a fool out of you, Gary.'

'Shut up, Des!' Gary grabbed him by the jacket and roared in his face. 'No one makes a fool outa me.'

'No?' Des swept his arms upwards in a single movement that broke Gary's grip. 'What's wrong with you –

scared? We should make sure O'Keefe gets what he deserves.'

Ruby's face turned the colour of her name. 'Ye'll get Gary locked up, so ye will. Call yerself a mate?'

'It's Gary's decision.'

'Yeah, *my* decision.'

Des had a plan all worked out. 'We won't get caught,' he said carefully, 'if you do exactly what I say. I'm thinking of something that'll keep you and me in the clear, Gary.'

'Like what?'

'Like getting help.'

'What kinda help?'

Des paused. 'Jimmy and Ben would sort him out for us.'

'No!' cried Ruby. 'Those two are lunatics!'

'But always happy to give a Fenian a good hiding! Isn't that so?'

Ruby gave Gary a little shake. 'This is pure mad – don't do it.'

Gary was chewing a knuckle, his eyes were round and bright, he was thinking hard. 'I wouldn't want to be in debt to that Ben,' he said. 'I only just kept me ribs intact last time we met. God know what he'd want in return for this.'

'We wouldn't be in debt,' said Des, ''cos we'd pay them.'

'*Pay them*? With what? I'm not into mugging old ladies and I haven't got that kind of cash, Des.'

'I have.'

Gary frowned. 'What's in this for you, Des?'

'Sorting out O'Keefe of course. You're me mate, Gary – we go back a long way.'

Ruby's eyes narrowed. 'Ye're up to something, Des Gordon – I know ye.'

Des glared at her, he had known she would cause trouble. 'Okay, so I want to get in touch with Jimmy and Ben again. So what? Gary blew it for me last time.'

'I'm not working for them again,' Gary muttered.

'You don't need to. But they'll do you a favour all the same – and *I* can get back in there. Make myself some decent money at last.'

'Yeah,' sneered Ruby. 'Ye lowlife – ye're just like them.'

Des clung onto his temper. 'I'm not going to sit around for the rest of my life watching Fenians move in on our girls! Well, Gary, what d'you say?'

'The cops will go straight to your door, Gary!'

'That's why we'll pay someone else to do the dirty work, stupid! Gary will have an alibi all sorted out.'

Gary was still hesitating, torn between the two of them. 'What if something goes wrong, Des? What if Tasha gets hurt?'

'You needn't worry about that! But those two will put the frighteners on Conor big time – he'll never want to go near a Protestant girl again.'

Ruby shook her head, her big hair streaming out around her. She was running out of arguments, she was losing Gary. 'Ye do this, Gary…then me and ye's finished.'

'What?' Gary looked as if she had slapped his face. 'Don't be ridiculous,' he said.

'I mean it. Come home wi' me, now. Do ye really want more trouble? 'Cos see me, I've had a gut full of it. Ye make up yer mind – it's me or Des.'

Gary stared at her. Stared as if they were communicating in some strange language. The bond between these two had always bugged Des, like rain trickling down his neck, irritating but impossible to stop. Suddenly Ruby flung away, her green Indian skirt swinging round her Doc Martens. Des didn't even realise he had been holding his breath until he let it go again. Gary had chosen and he had chosen *him*.

Gary shouted angrily up the street after her. 'You and me'll never finish, Ruby! There's too much between us!' He turned, glowering, to Des. 'So – what exactly is it you want me to do?'

The words sounded so sweet. Gary Proctor was asking him, Des Gordon, for orders. 'You leave things to me,' Des said coolly. 'I'll meet with Jimmy and Ben. After what happened there last time, you'd better steer clear. I'll fix it then let you know the details – all you need to do is get yourself an alibi.'

Gary lifted a foot and kicked the wall hard. 'I could have sorted this out myself, you know. I would have done if we hadn't got interrupted last night.'

'But now you can't. You've gotta keep your head down, that way you'll be in the clear – we both will.'

'Tasha mustn't get hurt, Des.'

'Trust me,' he said knowingly, 'Tasha will be fine.'

'She'd better be!' Gary was shouting, he was well rattled. 'I'm not into hurting women, you know.'

Des nearly laughed. He was starting to enjoy himself. Gary was too hot headed to be a leader. Gary had been top dog for far too long. Why didn't anyone realise it was him who kept his cool, not swaggering, good-looking Gary? It was time to teach Gary and his traitorous whore of a sister a lesson. Time to show them both who really called the shots.

Des got busy the very next morning when his mother went out to buy groceries. It took him half an hour to find the desk key, hidden, this time, on top of a pelmet. As he fumbled with the lock, the key slipped between his fingers and scratched the oak desk his mother was so fond of polishing. When he turned the key, water spilt out of the bowl of flowers on top, staining her precious antique.

Des pulled down the leaf and began rifling the desk. Where had she hidden her money this time? Among the bills and receipts? The guarantees and operating instructions? The birth certificates, passports and licences? Everything was so tidily filed in his mother's life that having to hide her money must infuriate her. She would far rather keep it in a shiny box neatly marked 'cash'.

Des searched all the pigeonholes and banged his way through the drawers underneath. The only photo of his father was kept there; a soft looking guy not quite facing the camera. Des tossed it away.

At the bottom of the third drawer, among the operating instructions for the vacuum cleaner, he found a hundred pounds. He pocketed it and went out of the back door as his mother came in the front.

Mrs Gordon put down her plastic carrier bags and discarded her grey cardigan with relief. It was far too hot for cardigans but she would never have dreamed of going sleeveless to the shops. Bare arms were for hussies.

She had carefully closed all the windows before she went out and the little house was stifling now. She crossed the living room to open the sash window and saw, with a little shock, the puddle of water staining her antique desk.

She ran into the kitchen, fetched a towel and mopped it up but it had left an ugly white stain. Mrs Gordon tut-tutted loudly then her eyes were drawn to the little scratches around the keyhole.

She knew instantly that Des was responsible. He had put the key back where he had found it. When she opened the desk she uttered a little cry.

He did not usually leave a mess. Her heart began beating like an injured sparrow's. Letters, bills and certificates were scattered all over the place, the pigeon-holes were emptied, the drawers chaotic. Mrs Gordon went straight to the operating instructions section of the desk and flicked through the vacuum cleaner documents, wondering if Des had left her anything at all.

There was nothing. Mrs Gordon looked helplessly around the room. She had used up all the hiding places now. Perhaps, in future, she would sew money into the curtain hems.

Something must have upset Des, she thought, to

create this mess. She decided that it would be better not to mention it to him, there was no point in upsetting him more.

Chaos. She looked at the papers strewn everywhere. It would take at least a couple of hours to sort it all out. Mrs Gordon set to work with determination.

The pub was dingy. There weren't many places like this left, even here in the heart of east Belfast. Tin ashtrays on small round tables, a bare bulb hanging over a darts board, a few ragged stools at the bar. It was a moment before Des's eyes adjusted to the darkness and when they did, he realised that everyone was looking at him. There were no women. The men, tattooed and overweight, stared at him suspiciously.

'Well, well,' Jimmy hailed him. 'If it isn't our pal from Hazel Grove.'

'Jimmy...Ben...I thought I'd find you here. How you doing?'

'We do okay. What brings you to these parts?'

Des slapped down a tenner on the bar. 'Three pints of Guinness, please.'

They drank at a dirty table, watching a game of darts.

'Where's your mate,' asked Ben. 'The bag o' nerves boy?'

'It's him I'm here about,' said Des, glad of the opening. 'Gary's got a bit of bother.'

'What kinda bother?' Ben looked at him over the top of his pint. 'Been shooting his mouth off again, has he?'

Des chose his words carefully. 'It's his sister. She's

been seeing a Fenian. Gary's tried to scare him off once already but it kinda backfired.'

'The wee bitch,' said Ben. His eyes glistened as if they were covered with a fine film of liquid paraffin.

'Their dad was killed by Fenians.'

'I remember you telling us,' said Jimmy. 'Copper, wasn't he?'

'Aye – and now this.'

Ben drained his pint and wiped the froth off his lips with a hairy forearm. 'So what is it you want from us?'

'Your help,' said Des lowering his voice. 'Gary's ma will get the police to him if he tries anything else – but you two could do it.'

'Do what exactly?'

Des took a deep breath; it was now or never. What was Zee thinking of, choosing that scummy Fenian instead of him? 'You could scare this Con O'Keefe off once and for all,' he said. 'Teach them both to stick to their own kind.'

Jimmy, supping his Guinness, said, 'It'd cost you more than a pint.'

Des fumbled with the money under the table and Jimmy counted it expertly out of sight.

'Daresay we could help,' he said, nodding at Ben.

'Be my pleasure.' Ben's face contorted in a big, gut-twisting smile. 'We need the details, Des. When? Where? How will we know them?'

Des's tongue felt hard and lifeless, like a piece of gum spat out and hardened on a pavement. He swallowed some beer, then he told them everything. Descriptions of

Conor and Zee. O'Keefe hadn't been seen around for a couple of days, he explained, but he couldn't hide for ever. The GCSE exam results were due out on the fifth of August. Des had found that out with a single phone call to the education department. O'Keefe was supposed to be a clever geek so he was sure to be out celebrating that night.

Des had no idea where they might go but he did know that Zee had to be home by midnight. She had told him so that night at the Co-op. That would put them in Hazel Grove anytime after half eleven. They'd probably come off the last bus.

Ben was nodding. 'My pleasure,' he said again and out of his boot he pulled a blade. A long, black-handled knife with a sharp, pitted blade.

Des felt his jaw drop. 'Bit heavy that,' he breathed.

'You told us O'Keefe's already been warned off once,' muttered Ben.

'I'm paying you to batter him – that's all.'

'Okay,' said Jimmy. 'What about the girl . . . in the old days she'd have been tarred and feathered.'

'Just give her a slap,' mumbled Des. 'Bring her back to her senses.' And hopefully, he thought, back to him.

Ben stared straight at him, his eyes glistening in his dark unshaven face. 'No way, Dessie boy,' he whispered.

Des broke into a sweat; it seeped from every pore in his body, soaked his hair, his clothes, everything. 'What do you mean?' he spluttered.

'She's a Fenian lover, isn't she? In spite of the fact they murdered her own father!' Ben's eyes and mouth widened venomously. 'I'll give her something she'll never be able to forget.'

Des met Ben's paraffin eyes again. Rumours came crowding back to him. Rumours half heard, half understood, like a game of Chinese whispers. Stories about Ben's girlfriend, blown to bits by an IRA bomb. About Ben spending the rest of his life getting even.

'Zee's only young,' Des said hoarsely. 'She doesn't understand what she's doing.'

'Then she needs to be taught.' Ben leaned towards him. 'You wouldn't be going soft on us would you, Des? Only we never work with soft buggers, know what I mean?'

'I'm one of you,' Des said fiercely. He looked at the big knife and swallowed hard. 'All the way.'

'Good.' Ben smiled his big terrifying smile again.

Maybe it was the heat or the dank, boozy atmosphere but Des knew that if he didn't get out of that pub right now he was going to keel over. Ben was playing with his knife again, stroking the hairline edge lovingly with his finger. As Des got to his feet, Ben made a swift jab.

'Aagh!'

Des's sleeve was pinned to the table. Ben turned the knife, screwing Des's sleeve right into the wood, bringing his face in so close that Des could smell the beer on his breath. No one in the pub even stirred.

'Remind me,' whispered Ben, 'what is it that happens to traitors and grasses, Des?'

Shaking with fear, Des gave him the answer he wanted.

'Punishment,' he said.

17

On beautiful summer days like this, Zee wondered how she would ever leave Ireland.

With the thermometer hitting eighty, her mother had packed up a picnic, piled them into the car and driven to the coast. After a swim they retreated, for the hottest part of the day, to the shade of Tullymore Forest. Now, lazing on the grass, Zee watched sunlight shoot like lasers between the trees and millions of tiny particles caught in the sunbeams danced and spun. The giant pines looked more stately and aloof than ever in this heat, and the little lough looked calmer, darker, even more mysterious.

Zee told herself firmly that there were beautiful places the world over, *But not your places*, whispered a voice in her head. *Not this place*.

'You okay, Mum?' she asked, determined to vanquish her own thoughts.

'Yes, I think I am.' She sounded surprised.

'Thanks for the ice cream.'

It had been a special ice cream. Another First. Last summer the Proctors had made a great effort and forced themselves back to the coast – all except Gary. But they had not, could not, bring themselves to visit the sea-front shop where Dad used to buy big frothy ice creams with stick-up chocolate flakes. Today Sue had driven straight there, marched in without a word and emerged with five ices and not a single tear.

'It has got easier,' she said to Zee.

'Good.'

'For a long time I didn't even *want* it to get easier, you know.'

Zee glanced at her mother nervously. It had been such a lovely day; surely she wasn't going to get all heavy and sentimental now?

But she went on talking. 'I couldn't stop thinking about your dad at first, not for months and months. Not when I was awake anyway, and often not when I was sleeping either.' She laughed unexpectedly. 'It was so exhausting! Then, when he did, occasionally, begin to slip from my thoughts, I felt disloyal.'

'You shouldn't have. Dad wouldn't want you to grieve for ever.'

'I know that, I knew it then too. But your heart doesn't always do what your head tells you.'

'No,' murmured Zee, thinking about Conor, 'it doesn't.'

'Grief chews you up, it leaves you going forever backwards, over and over things all the time. But I think I'm starting to move forward again now – even if I am just crawling along in first gear! Do you understand me?'

Zee nodded although she wasn't completely sure that she did.

'How about you, love?'

'You know me, I'm fine. Shall we have the picnic now?'

Her mother reached over and squeezed her hand. 'You know, sometimes I think it affected you worst of all.'

'Me?' Zee stared at her in amazement. 'What on earth do you mean?'

'No one should grieve for ever, love, but we all need to do it sometime.'

Zee sat up abruptly. It was as if someone had struck a match in her stomach and a harsh little flame flared up. 'You think I haven't?' she demanded.

'Not fully, no.'

The flicker of anger grew bigger and bigger, she thought she would burst into flames with a whoosh. 'Get off!' she cried, pulling away from her mother's hand.

'Zee, I didn't mean—'

'You're so unfair! I wasn't the one who went to pieces. It was you and Gary who went all flaky! Someone had to stay sensible. Who would have looked after the twins if I hadn't?'

'You were wonderful. I'm just—'

'No!' Zee stuck her fingers in her ears. 'You know I don't like talking about it.' She stood up. 'Twins! Tasha! Come and get some food.'

They arrived, feet first, among the picnic.

'Watch what you're doing!' Zee yelled. 'You've put tread-marks on the sandwiches, you eejits! Get off.'

'We were only having a race,' said Josh.

'Has Zee gone mad with the sun?' asked Gemma but nobody answered.

'I need lemonade,' declared Josh. 'I'm dying of thirst.'

'Wee sausages!' whooped Gemma, diving for a tupperware box.

'Wait! Look at the pair of you – you've streaming

noses. Trust my kids to catch colds in summer. Blow those noses and wipe your hands on the Wet Ones before you touch a thing.'

'Aiachoo!'

Still edgy, Zee lay back in the sun and Tasha flopped down beside her, sweaty and red in the face.

'That was hard work,' she panted. 'I didn't appreciate how demanding being a goalkeeper is.'

'Goalie,' Josh corrected her. 'Actually, you weren't bad for a girl goalie.'

'Compliment accepted,' said Tasha solemnly. 'I don't think I've played football before.'

'No,' snorted Zee, 'you had to make do with lacrosse, summer balls and holidays all over Europe.'

Tasha stared at her in surprise.

'People can miss the simple things,' said her mum quietly.

For no reason at all, an image flashed into Zee's mind. Her dad, his curly blond hair flopping forward, playing rough-tumble with them on the couch. Her mum, shrieking about the springs as they all piled on, bashing each other with cushions, and tickling tummies and feet and whatever else they could get hold of until Mum gave over complaining and joined in too. Zee shook her head, flicking the memory away like dust. What was wrong with her today? Was it the heat? The setting? Her mum's weird ideas?

'I'll tell you what,' she said, 'when I'm a famous war correspondent miles and miles away from here, I'll remember the simple things in life and bring my kids back home for holidays. How's that?'

'Are you calling me simple?' teased her mum.

They grinned at each other and Zee knew that everything was back to normal. After lunch she and Tasha hired rowing boats, put a twin in each, and raced up and down the lough. They played volleyball and hide-and-seek and cricket. Later, with the twins running ahead and Sue left behind to enjoy some peace, they wandered along a cool forest trail.

'Are you still on for this party tonight?' asked Zee. 'I could do with a bit of fun.'

'I'm not sure. The party's at Tracy's, isn't it? I don't know Tracy.'

'Yes, you do. She's in my class. I introduced you on the eleventh night, remember? You've had days to think about it, Tasha – I got the invite a week ago.'

'I'm not into parties at the moment.'

'You're not into anything at the moment.'

'You calling me boring?'

'Well...do you remember that promise we made the first day we met?'

'Of course I do – to make the most of this summer.' Tasha pulled a face. 'Now summer's half over and my one romance was a disaster.'

'There's still time for another.'

'Yeah – another disaster too.'

'Come on, Tasha. We've read, we've watched telly. We've taken the twins to the park, swimming, the cinema...and Saturday is still three whole days away!'

'All right – but no guzzling alcohol this time.'

Zee gasped. 'That was *your* idea.'

'I'll take a red hanky. If I want to leave, or I'm getting hassled, I'll pretend to blow my nose with it.'

'What if you catch the twins' colds? You might need to use it a lot.'

'I'm serious, Zee. I've done some thinking, you know. One thing I've learned this summer is to get in control of my social life.'

'Really?'

'Really.'

'You know, when we first met, Tasha, I thought you were totally sorted.'

'Whatever do you mean?'

'Because of your posh school, I suppose, and your rich dad. I thought you'd be...I dunno...dead experienced.'

Tasha laughed. 'Then you realised you'd never met anyone quite so naive or anyone who can mess things up quite as spectacularly as I can.'

'Correct. Ouch!' Tasha had punched her playfully on the shoulder. 'Do you realise that it's weeks since I've seen Conor?'

'Now who's being boring?'

'Eh?'

'It wasn't too bad the first fifty times you mentioned him but now...I've got to get away!'

Tasha raced off and Zee chased her along the forest track. Eventually, tired out, they all collapsed on the grass again, back at base with Sue, and Tasha treated everyone to a second ice cream.

'What a pity Gary didn't come with us,' said Sue, sighing. 'Then it really would have been a perfect day.

'Er... what is he doing today?' asked Tasha.

'Mooching, I expect,' said Zee. 'Gary is an expert moocher – up and down the Newtownards Road, all around Hazel Grove, and he's *particularly* skilled at mooching behind the Co-op.'

'Don't be so hard on your brother. He promised to fix my fountain today.'

'That statue must be dying for a pee by now,' said Gemma and she and Josh both howled with laughter, smearing ice cream all over their faces.

'Can't wait to see that in operation again,' groaned Zee.

'At least Gary's *trying*,' said her mum forcefully.

'Trying... to act less like a caveman?' Tasha giggled. 'Doing less wall-painting perhaps?'

Sue bristled. 'Gary thinks the world of you, Tasha. That graffiti was childish and unforgivable, but the truth is that he can't bear to think of you going out with someone else.'

Tasha blushed and Zee could not look at either of them. All these lies, all this deception... all for *her*. She was just about to wander off when her mother called her back.

'I've got something to tell you all,' she announced. She sounded almost shy but there was an excitement about her too. 'You know I've been thinking about going back to work? Well... I've decided what I'm going to do.'

'What?' they asked in unison.

'I'm going to become a teacher.'

Zee gasped and the twins must have been just as gob-smacked because even they were silenced.

'It'll fit nicely round the family because I'll be home by four o'clock, and I'll have the same holidays as you do.'

'Why teaching?' asked Tasha.

'It's a worthwhile job.'

'No, it isn't!' Josh jumped up and raced around, his arms flailing and his tongue lashing. 'Teachers are dragons!'

'I am not a dragon and I never will be.'

'Aren't you too old?' asked Zee.

Her mother shot her a look that would have withered a beanstalk, and then pulled a newspaper cutting from her pocket. 'This is about an information evening next Saturday for people who want to do teacher training. It's a social do. I thought I'd go along.'

Zee felt a horrible panicky jolt. 'This Saturday?' The GCSE results were coming out this Saturday. It would be the first time in over two weeks that she would see Conor. What would he think if she didn't show up? 'Not this Saturday, Mum, I can't babysit then.'

'Er – Mum's dinner party's that night,' Tasha put in helpfully. 'Remember we told you about it, Sue? Zee's invited.'

'Gary's going to babysit.'

'*Gary*?' Zee gasped again. 'When did Gary last babysit?'

'He was very obliging when I asked him, and *he* doesn't think I'm too old for teaching.'

'I thought you had to be born a teacher,' said Gemma, 'like a farmer's born a farmer.'

'Not always, darling.'

'Good, can I be a farmer then, Mum?'

Tasha grinned. 'I think you'll make a fantastic teacher, Sue. At least you like kids – half our teachers don't. I've seen you out in the garden playing hide-and-seek with the twins, reading them stories, showing them flowers – you'll be great.'

'Thanks for the vote of confidence, Tasha. Well, Zee? It should mean we can afford a few more glad-rags.'

'I think it's amazing . . . brilliant.' Zee gave her mother a hug. 'Just one thing,' she said solemnly. 'Promise never to teach in my school.'

Tracy's party was just as Tasha had feared. Three rooms full to bursting with loud music, spilt drinks and sixteen-year-old boys all after the same thing. At first she and Zee stayed in the kitchen, sipping punch and nibbling cheesy things on crackers. School friends were busy catching up on news and holiday romances in the sun. Tasha was made welcome but after an hour she was glad to escape to the drawing room to dance.

She and Zee danced together at first but two guys soon interrupted them. Zee's guy looked fit but Zee wasn't interested. Tasha's had the physique of a pin. The music was good though and for a while she let herself go, enjoying the sounds and the semi-dark and the sight of so many other people into the same thing.

When they stopped, Pin-man said, 'Wait here.'

177

Charming, thought Tasha, and watched him totter unsteadily towards the kitchen. She tried to mingle but it wasn't easy to lose herself in such a confined space and he was back a few minutes later with two plastic cups slopping punch. By the look of him, he had drunk a couple more in the kitchen.

'What's your name?' she shouted above the music.

'Bob.' He grabbed her hand. 'Come with me.'

Tasha thought about her red hanky but she couldn't see Zee anywhere. She let Bob lead her into the other room where all the lights were out. Three clutching couples occupied the settee, and others were draped round armchairs and curtains. The floor was a mass of moaning couples and the air was stale with smoke and sweat.

'Er...I'm not sure—' she began.

But Bob's mouth was on top of hers already. He was like a dog gnawing at a bone, slavering all over her, trying to devour her all at once. Tasha pulled away crossly.

'Whassamatter?' he asked, focusing with obvious difficulty. 'Jeez, you're gorgeous.'

He fell on top of her and this time his hands were everywhere, fumbling with her blouse, her skirt, grabbing at her thigh. 'Will you – um – will you go wi' me? Will you?'

'I've never seen you before,' said Tasha. She could feel him pressing against her hip and she nearly panicked.

'Stop it!' she hissed.

'Whassamatter?' he said again.

Time to get out. She didn't want to humiliate him, but there was no way she was going to be humiliated again.

'*You're* whassamatter,' she said. 'By – ye!'

It was as easy as that. She had been so worried about this, so scared, but when it happened, she just slid out and walked away. Tasha felt terrific; totally sorted, totally in charge.

She left the room, went back into the kitchen and joined a group of girls. An hour later, after Zee had caught up with her friends and Tasha had danced a good bit more, they left and walked home together.

'No red hanky signals,' noted Zee, yawning.

'No.'

'You looked like you were enjoying yourself.'

Tasha smiled as she turned in at her gate. She could not begin to describe how good she felt. The relief, after all these weeks, of proving she could cope. How could she tell Zee who coped with everything, who took life completely in her stride, who let nothing, not Conor, not Gary, not even her own father's death, get in her way?

Zee was going to be a top-flight journalist and Tasha felt quite sure that she would make it.

Zee was smart, Zee was pretty.

Zee could be anything she wanted.

18

Zee perched on the linen basket, lipstick in hand and peered in the bathroom mirror. The casual look she was trying so hard to achieve seemed terribly complicated. Holding her breath she smudged lipstick across her cheeks then applied it to her lips. Iced Sunset it was called. She had picked up the trick from Tasha who said that lipstick and blusher should match exactly because an even tone flatters. So why, Zee wondered, did Iced Sunset make her look like one of those over-the-top cosmetics assistants from Boots? She surveyed her eye make-up gloomily. According to Tasha and the teen magazines, she should use four different shades on her upper eyelid alone. But how? Where? Her eyelid wasn't big enough. As for eyeliner, that hurt. Perhaps a little mascara, on the upper lashes only...

'Zee!' shrieked a voice.

She got such a fright that she poked her eye with the mascara wand. She hurried downstairs, rubbing it as she went. 'What's the panic, Mum?'

'Gemma's got a temperature – that's what – and *I* should have left by now.'

'So she has,' said Zee, feeling her sister's hot little forehead. 'You poor wee thing.'

'How come *she* gets all the fuss?' demanded Josh. 'My head hurts too.'

'Because *she's* got spots,' said Gary.

'Spots?' Zee couldn't help having a go at Gary who was standing in the chintzy bay window with his arms firmly crossed. 'So that's why you're keeping a safe distance – my hero!'

'Be quiet, you two – what spots are you talking about?' Their mother pulled Gemma's hair away from her ears for a closer look. Gemma promptly burst into tears.

'I don't want spots. I'll look horrible with spots. No one will ever marry me!'

'Eejit!' Zee gave her sister a hug. 'They'll fade away. Sure you've only just got – um?'

'Plague?' suggested Gary.

'Chicken pox,' said their mum. 'It isn't a cold these two have had lately, they've been incubating chicken pox.'

'Shouldn't we call a doctor?' asked Gary. 'To give them jabs?'

Gemma screamed and Zee had to stop Josh doing a runner. Sue glowered at her oldest son.

'No doctor and no jabs,' she said firmly. 'We just need to keep them quiet, give them Calpol every six hours and lots to drink in between.' She glanced at her watch and groaned. 'I might have known that as soon as I even *thought* about going out to work you kids would fall ill. I'd better cancel.'

'No,' said Zee firmly. 'This evening's important for you, Mum. You go – Gary will cope.'

'Me? On me own? Cope with the two of them *and* the chicken pox? What about you, sunshine?'

Zee gritted her teeth; there was no way Gary was stopping her going out now. 'I've made arrangements too,' she said, 'and I can't change them.'

'It's only a flamin' tea-party.'

'It's dinner! A posh dinner with four courses and VIPs. And I've promised Tasha I'll be there.' Zee felt herself turn redder with every lie. At least their mother seemed to have made up her mind; she was picking up her car keys.

'Right, I'll ring as soon as I get to the teaching college,' she said. 'If these two are feeling worse I'll just grab some leaflets and come straight back. Gary, give them plenty of Coke – it'll stop them dehydrating.'

'What about her?' he demanded.

'Zee will be just across the road if you need her. Won't you, love?'

Zee swallowed hard. 'Yeah, 'course I will.'

Gary was still scowling at her, his eyes narrowed. 'Don't get too comfortable, party girl, 'cos if I need you, I'll be straight on that phone.'

Praying that she would not be needed, Zee picked up her bag and fled.

Conor had got to the bookshop first. He was waiting in the fantasy section right by the front door, his hands in his pockets, his dark hair flopping forward as he read the titles. Zee's stomach spun like a coin. He was so good looking and so much fun; was he really hers?

Suddenly, unexpectedly, she wavered. What good could possibly come of this relationship? If *only* he wasn't Catholic. Maybe she should get out before she got in any deeper. After all, if she didn't show up tonight, Conor would understand. He would know that it was too risky for her, too hard. Sure, he'd be disappointed, but he would go home and gradually get over it and they would both be safe. Maybe she should walk away right now.

'Conor?' she whispered.

He raced to her and wrapped her up in his arms, tightly, so very, very tightly, as if he was never ever going to let her go again, as if she meant everything to him, his entire world.

'I've missed you so much!' He kissed her head, her face, her neck, not caring what anyone in the shop might think. 'I thought I was going mad without you. How did I ever get a girl like you? I *love* you, Zee.'

She looked up and only silenced him by putting her finger on his lips. Conor started laughing.

'What's happened, Zee? Did you fall in the coal bucket?'

Too late she remembered the accident with the mascara, then, with horror, she saw his blue shirt, a new shirt by the look of it, streaked with black. 'Oh no, Con!'

But he just laughed louder and picked her up and spun her round and everyone in Bookbinder's stared at them all over again.

'I'm going to get cleaned up, Con – five minutes.'

In the Ladies, Zee scrubbed off all the make-up and was about to start again when she decided not to. Conor loved her, this face staring back at her, naked, from the mirror.

She loved him too and if they had to explain exactly what it was they loved about each other, maybe they couldn't. Maybe that was what made it all so exciting.

Her eyes twinkled at her in the mirror, her teeth gleamed and her newly washed hair had sparkling gold highlights. Perhaps she didn't look so bad after all. She would never have flawless skin or fantastically long legs but she looked happy and healthy and Conor loved her.

Zee threw the make-up back in her bag and found him waiting at an alcove table. They held hands around the single candle and talked quickly. The waiter bringing their coffees had to cough to catch their attention.

'Come on, tell me your results, Con.'

'I did okay,' he said modestly. 'Got eight.'

Zee barked with delight. 'Good grades?'

'Good enough for medicine.'

'That means they're brilliant.'

Conor allowed himself a grin. 'S'pose so... straight As actually.'

'Conor!' She flung her arms around him. 'Clever, clever you!'

'I'm doing physics, chemistry and biology for A level.' His eyes started to shine. 'Zee, this means that one day, I really *could* be a surgeon, you know.'

'What did your folks say?'

He laughed. 'It's stopped them going on about Gary and the fight – that's the main thing.'

'I bet they were delighted.'

'Yeah, they treated me to this shirt.'

184

She delved into her bag. 'I've brought you something too. It's not much but I did it myself.'

His smooth features set with curiosity as he balanced the little parcel in the palm of his hand. 'It's heavy.'

'No guessing – open it.'

Conor stripped off the red paper to reveal a pure white stone intricately painted in black with a Celtic design of two bodies entwined.

'Us,' he breathed, tracing the winding pattern with a finger.

'I picked up the stone at Helen's Bay the night of the party.'

'It's stunning, Zee. I didn't know you could paint.'

'Sure it's only wiggly lines,' she said but inside she was glowing with pleasure.

'It's much more than that.' His soft eyes searched hers. 'This will sit on the mantelpiece of our first flat,' he whispered.

Zee felt panic flooding through her body like a lock-gate opening on a canal. Her head emptied of any sensible response and she started jabbering about chicken pox and Tullymore forest and Tracy's party while all the time her mind was racing with other thoughts.

Their first flat? Why had he gone and said that? What was the point of leaping ahead? Weren't things complicated enough already?

When Bookbinder's closed they moved on to a pizza hut, ate huge pizzas and toasted Conor's success with Coke. She told him about her mother's information evening and he told her about a spectacular skate-boarding

185

accident one of his brothers had been involved in, and they both carefully avoided the subject of themselves.

'Kieran said it was his best accident yet,' laughed Conor. 'My old man's on at me to take it up now.'

'You're far too old,' she said deflatingly. 'You have to be about twelve to skate-board.'

'I know. Ach, he's just trying to keep me out of trouble.'

'Away from Tasha, you mean.' Zee groaned heavily. 'Away from me – if only he knew it.'

'Now don't go all gloomy.'

'It's the lying I hate, Con. What are we going to do?'

He stroked her bare arm. 'Don't worry, we'll be okay. There's a kinda peace, isn't there? One day we'll be able to go public. Couples like us are going to be just fine.'

Zee moved her arm away slowly. Sometimes she felt older than Conor, and wiser, despite all his brains. 'Have you forgotten Gary?' she asked him.

'If Gary's bitter, that's his problem.'

'But it's mine too. Can't you understand? I lost my dad – I couldn't bear to lose the rest of my family too.'

Conor sat back slowly in his chair, his face tightening up. 'What are you trying to say, Zee? Don't you think we've got a future then?'

'Don't go all cold on me, Con.'

'Well, what exactly are you trying to say?'

'Just that Gary's never going to let us set up home together.'

'He can't stop us.'

'Aye, he can – he could split my family over it.'

'That's their choice. Zee, do you love me or don't you?'

186

'Would I be here if I didn't? Would I be lying to my whole family and making Tasha lie too?'

'Then what's the problem?'

'I want *all* of you – I don't want to have to choose between you and them.' Suddenly an idea flitted through her head like a bat through an attic and she blurted it out. 'We could go to London and get a flat there, just the two of us – then nobody need know!'

'Don't be ridiculous,' he said scathingly. 'How would we keep a thing like that a secret?'

'We could if we tried hard enough.' She knew she was chasing a rainbow but she couldn't stop babbling. 'I could join a newspaper, you could do your A levels at college—'

'Whoa! I'm not going anywhere.'

'But it might be the only way we could make it work.'

'It wouldn't!' His eyes flashed at her. 'This is our home, Zee. *Belfast.* I'm not going to be chased away by Gary or by anyone else. I've told you, I'm going to be part of the peace – and so should you.'

'Don't tell me what I should do,' she retaliated. 'So you want to be part of the peace, do you? Huh! Where does knocking the shit out of Gary fit into that peace plan?'

'Smart ass.'

'Hypocrite! Hypocrisy's half the problem with this country. I've told you before, I'm getting out of here as fast as I can.'

'Off you go then – run away!'

'I'm *not* running away.'

'Aye, y'are. Want to know why? 'Cos you're scared,

Zee – scared of your own family!'

Anger made her shake all over. The sort of anger that comes with the awful realisation that someone you've allowed to get close knows you better than you know yourself.

'I have to leave Ireland,' she shouted at him, 'I have to!'

How else could she get away from Gary's anger and Sue's tears? Free herself from the men stamping up and down in orange sashes, clinging to dates in history books. Or be free of the gunmen who had murdered her dad, men who were walking the same streets as her? Sitting, maybe, at the very next table? Why *should* she live with any of it? How could she bear to?

Suddenly Conor was right there, his arms around her. Only then did she realise she was crying.

'Zee, I'm sorry, I shouldn't have said that. You're the bravest person I know.' His voice was shaking. 'Why are we arguing? I've been looking forward to tonight for so long. I'm so *so* sorry.'

'Me too.' She gulped back the tears. 'Can't we just carry on how we were?'

'I wasn't planning on dragging you off to bedsit land yet. It's just—' He broke off and kissed her tenderly. 'For a moment, I caught a wee glimpse of how things could be – one day. Is a shared mantelpiece too much to hope for?'

She gazed at him through her tears. Life had been so straightforward two months ago. She had known exactly what she wanted then.

'Oh, Con,' she whispered, 'why did I have to fall for you?'

19

'C'mon, Gemma,' coaxed Gary, 'you heard Mum – you've gotta drink.'

'Yuck!' said Gemma.

'But Coke's your favourite – all those E numbers – I've even put ice in it.'

'Yuck!' she said again and turned her head.

Gary could see beads of sweat strung out across her forehead. He fetched a flannel soaked in cold water and laid it across her brow like they did in the old black and white war movies. In those, the patients gasped gratefully, but Gemma just flung the flannel back at him.

'Sod you,' he said.

Josh was flaked out on two armchairs Gary had shoved together, surrounded by videos and comics. Gary punched his arm playfully. 'How you doing, wee man?'

'Aow! What did you do that for, you big bully?'

Gary groaned. He just wasn't cut out to be Florence Nightingale.

'I feel sick,' said Josh.

'Don't you dare!'

Josh retched and Gary ran for a bowl. By the time he got back Josh had thrown up all over the carpet.

'What a stink! Could you not hold on, Josh?'

'I want my mum,' Gemma started whining from the couch.

Gary held his nose with one hand and used the coal shovel to lift the biggest bits of vomit off the carpet. He tossed them onto the fire and carrot and celery sizzled on the coals. Then he fetched the Dettol and poured about a pint of it over the stain on the carpet, rubbing it in with his trainer.

'That smell's going to make me sick again,' Josh told him.

Gary opened the window, then he built up the fire again. Was he supposed to keep them warm or keep them cool? And how could he make Gemma drink if she didn't want to? At least Josh was drinking.

'I'm going to be sick again,' Josh announced.

This time Gary caught it in the bowl though he had to turn his face away, screwed up in disgust. Josh lay back, white-faced, asking pathetically for his mum.

She had rung earlier but the kids had been all right then. The moment he had reassured her and put the phone down they started getting worse. She would be on her way home by now but the traffic could be bad at closing time on a Saturday night.

Gary's stomach leapt. A quarter past eleven. How could he have forgotten?

He pressed his face against the cold windowpane and craned his neck. Right at the top of the hill a car was parked, a big pale saloon, lying there, nose first, like some killer fish.

It must be them. What if Des had messed things up? What if they beat up the wrong guy? Gary's stomach started squeezing in and out like a juicer. Maybe he

190

should sprint up to the car and cancel the whole thing.

But O'Keefe deserved a good doing, didn't he? Something to warn him off properly. Tasha was safely with her mum and Zee tonight, and he and Des had sound alibis. He mustn't lose his bottle.

'I want my mummy,' demanded Gemma.

'Well you can't have her,' he said.

'Zee then. Zee knows what to do.'

'And I don't? Thanks a bunch.'

Still, maybe it was not such a bad idea. Zee might know if they should be kept hot or cool. She might even know how to keep fluids down them. And it was her turn to hold the sick bowls. 'I'll ring her,' he announced.

At first no one answered. Probably drunk, or else that creepy Bosnian was deafening them all with his piano. Gary had heard him banging away at it before, loud enough to drive out evil.

'Hello,' came a voice at last.

'Tasha?' He broke into a sweat just talking to her down the phone. 'How's things?'

'Gary? Hi. Things are fine.'

'Good – er – I need to speak to Zee.'

There was a crackling noise. 'Er... bad line. Shall I... take a message?'

'Tell her to come home.'

'Home?' Tasha sounded stunned.

'The place she's supposed to live?'

'Yeah – um – it's just that we... haven't had coffee yet.'

'Too bad! She's needed.' Gary was irritated. 'Her wee brother and sister are at death's door.'

191

There was more crackling, then Tasha promised to send Zee home and the line went dead.

When Gary went back into the living room things had got even worse. Josh was complaining tearfully about being itchy then Gemma started throwing up too. Gary held the bowl for her but when some of it splashed onto his thumb he thought he was going to be sick himself.

'Don't scratch,' he yelled at Josh. 'If you scratch you'll have scars. No one wants scars, do they?'

Josh started crying for real now, howling for his mother. Where had she got to? And where was Zee? It was only a two-minute walk from Tasha's.

'Where's Zee?' moaned Gemma. 'I want *Zee.*'

Her face was flushed and shiny, she looked really ill. Gary gritted his teeth. He would have to go and drag Zee home. The selfish cow. Too bad if it embarrassed her, she should have come back when he rang.

'Right, you two – don't move,' he instructed. 'I'm going to get Zee.'

He shot out of the house and along the road. The big car had just started cruising. Tasha opened the front door to him almost at once.

'Hi,' she said breezily.

'Where's Zee?'

'She's coming.'

'Good.' He couldn't help eyeing Tasha up as he waited. A slinky black dress clung to her curves and her hair was piled on top of her head with blonde tendrils trailing sexily down. The sounds of tinkling glass and laughter came from inside. 'Is she coming or do I have to go in and get her?' he demanded.

'Please don't! Look, you go back and I'll make sure Zee follows.'

'She's needed *now*. The twins are chuckin' up all over the place.'

There was a movement inside but instead of Zee, it was Magda who appeared, dressed in red and silver. 'Hello – it's Gary, isn't it?'

'Yes, I've come for Zee,' he said politely.

'Oh, but Zee's not here. She told us weeks ago she couldn't make it tonight, didn't she, Tasha?' Magda winked. 'Other fish to fry, I suspect.'

Gary looked at Tasha but Tasha had closed her eyes. She seemed to be praying. Magda went back to her party but Gary grabbed Tasha's wrist before she could follow. He pulled her down the steps and out of earshot.

'What the hell's going on, Tash?'

'Nothing!'

'Where is she?'

'I don't know.'

'You *do*. You girls tell each other everything.'

Tasha's chin shot up defiantly. 'Yeah? Well it's none of your business, you big bully!'

That was the second time he'd been called a bully tonight, he thought bitterly. 'Is it some biker or something? Some punk me mum wouldn't like?'

But Tasha didn't answer, she just stared at him boldly, even when he yelled right in her face. Suddenly Gary twigged. 'It's someone *I* wouldn't like, isn't it?'

A screech of brakes split the night air at that moment,

followed by another screech, then car doors banged and there was shouting.

'Whatever's that?' cried Tasha.

'Nothing!' Suddenly his heart jolted like a bungee jumper's. 'Where is Zee? Who's she with, Tasha – *tell me*!'

At that moment Gary heard his sister scream.

20

On the bus home, Conor and Zee had cuddled up. He kissed her more tenderly than ever, cradling her face between his hands and brushing her lips gently with his own.

'There are so many things I should have said tonight,' he whispered.

'There's no need,' she whispered back and it was true. She could make out every word just by looking in his eyes; she had never seen them so soft and loving.

'I can't believe we argued,' he murmured.

But they had. Nothing could close this chasm that had opened up between them, thought Zee. Conor would stay in his Brave New Ireland and she would not.

The problem had always been there, like a crack in the ground beneath them, but tonight something volcanic had opened up that crack and thrust them apart. Zee did not think things would ever be quite the same again.

At Hazel Grove the last of the day's heat hung, heavy as a dust-sheet, over the leafy suburb. Gardens exuded a sickly heightened perfume, and overhead, trees flung out their branches like thirsty wraiths, sucking at the darkness underneath.

Zee shivered in spite of the heat, she would be glad to get home. As they strode out she heard the low cough of an ignition and saw a car move slowly towards them. One gear change instead of two.

'Why's it creeping along, Con?'

He didn't answer. His hand tightened around hers and as the car drew level, he muttered, 'Keep walking!'

Her heart missed a beat. The two men inside it stared out at them, then accelerated smoothly away.

'Who d'you think they are, Con?'

'Dunno.' His face was taut and he gripped her hand so tightly that it hurt. 'Let's nip into the woods, Zee, just in case.'

She didn't ask in case of what, she was too scared. They left the pavement and ran for the trees.

'Watch out, Zee!'

Lights blazing, accelerating hard, the car came swarming back. They leapt back onto the pavement just in time. Brakes screeched as the car swerved in a tight U-turn, then sped back, rocking to a halt just feet away.

The doors flew open. Blinded by the beam, Conor and Zee picked out two men, hooded now and black as rocks against the headlights.

One came towards them, moving like a statue with one arm outstretched. A blade glinted in his hand.

'No ...' It was Conor's voice, Zee's had vanished altogether. Conor's came again, stronger this time. 'It's me you want – not her. D'you hear? Leave her be!'

A fist in his mouth answered him as the second man moved in. Conor's hand was torn from Zee's as he went tumbling over backwards.

Alone now, the blade came glinting towards her. Behind it eyes glittered through holes in a balaclava. Bright cruel eyes. Zee's stomach folded up with dread.

The man grabbed her sweatshirt with his free hand and forced her to the ground. It happened so fast, seemed so astonishing, that she didn't even yell. It was only when he knelt on her stomach, crushing her body that she felt pain. She began to gasp for breath. For one moment she thought she would be raped.

'No...no...please don't...'

Perhaps it was hearing herself beg, perhaps it was Conor's cries as he was kicked, but somewhere, deep inside Zee, something clicked. Out of her shock emerged the urgent, overwhelming need to get away, to get help, to save them both, to run like she had never run before.

She started to fight back. She writhed beneath the man, jerking and twisting her body. She tried to wrench away, battering him with her fists and thrashing him with her feet. Her fingers hurt she gripped him so hard, even her nails ached. But gradually, terrifyingly, her limbs lost strength.

It was hopeless. His sheer size and strength defeated her. He let her struggle until she was reduced to exhausted feeble spasms, as helpless as a fly in a Venus trap.

'Fenian lover,' he croaked at her. 'Bitch! This is for your da.'

For one moment he held the blade flat and cold against her cheek. Their eyes met and his glittered suddenly, like crushed ice. Behind the balaclava he had smiled. Then the knife bit and tore across her cheek.

'Oh dear God, no!' It was Conor's voice filled with disbelief.

Zee's cheek punctured like a summer apple but it took

a moment for the skin to separate and pull apart. Long enough for Zee to think that perhaps, somehow, bizarrely, it would be okay. Then she felt her blood begin to seep and drip. It soaked into her mouth. Repulsed, she spat it out. Blood clogged her nostrils so she could barely breathe. A slick of it glued her eyes.

Fear came roaring back as the knife cut again, fear like a hundred-foot wave threatening to drown her. She heard herself screaming, then she knew that she had to hold on. She braced herself like a surfer clinging to life, against that huge, annihilating panic.

Somehow she held on. Saw her own blood splatter the pavement but held on. Saw his hairy wrist flick before her eyes, smelt the stench of sweat and beer coming off him, but held on. It would stop eventually if only she held on.

'Ben!' shouted someone. 'Get off her! Leave her be!'

It was Gary. Unbelievably, Gary.

'Help!' she screamed at him. 'Help me, Gary!'

'Jimmy, call him off – he's lost it!'

There was panic in her brother's voice. Blood blinded her, she could see nothing but she knew it was Gary who tore into her assailant because she recognised his gasp. Then came sudden staggering release. The man had thrown her aside, there was more shouting, then doors banged and the car screeched off.

She flinched as arms went round her once more but this time they were Gary's arms. 'It's over,' he said. 'It's over, it's over.' And he kept saying it while the moments passed and she began to believe that it was true.

There were more running footsteps, high-heeled running, then Tasha's voice as clear and English as Big Ben.

'Oh my God, no! Stay where you are – don't move. I'll get help.'

Her heels clattered off again and Zee felt someone gently wiping her eyes.

'Open them,' pleaded Conor, 'please, *please* open your eyes, Zee.'

She struggled to separate her eyelids. At first she couldn't, then they came apart like a torn seam and the first thing she saw was Conor, kneeling in front of her, using his new shirt to clean her eyes. Heavens, his mother would kill him.

'I can see,' she whispered, 'I *can* see.'

Gary was still at her side, still holding her up ... Gary, tear-streaked, so white and shocked she hardly knew him. And yet she did ... Gary, swagger gone, stripped back to being her brother.

Conor, bloodied and bruised, rounded on him. 'You knew their names, Gary ... you *knew*!'

'I ...' Gary shook his head but he didn't deny it and his eyes were wild. 'This wasn't meant to happen,' he said. 'I swear it wasn't!'

Conor let out a roar like a lion and he might have torn Gary limb from limb if feet had not come running from all directions and suddenly there were neighbours fussing, lights flashing, someone pressing buttons on a mobile phone.

'Go, Gary,' breathed Zee, then she found herself so weak that she could hardly speak.

'What?' he pressed. '*What did you say?*'

Conor understood. 'She's telling you to disappear – before the police arrive.'

'But—'

'Then do us all a favour,' said Conor fiercely, 'and stay disappeared.'

Something shut down deep inside Zee's head. Some part of her tried to move to a place where there was no fuss and no noise and no difficult decisions to be made. Voices floated around her but they were unreal, disembodied voices like echoes, and she didn't have to answer echoes.

'... keep her awake,' said one echo.

'... lost a lot of blood,' came another.

'... what sort of beast would do this?' Unmistakably Mrs G.

Zee's head spun further and further away. Darkness moved in from the edges, floating dizzily, sickeningly, swallowing her up.

'Hang on, Zee, talk to me!'

She wanted to answer Con and to take him with her. Wherever she was going, she desperately wanted him to be there.

A shrieking siren brought her back for a moment, she saw flashing lights and people moving about. Sounds came and went with brittle, elongated echoes and she had the weird sensation of spinning away from them all. Nothing to hold on to, gravity pulling her down, tearing at her, forcing her away. And finally a huge glass globe shattering all around her as her grip loosened and she went spinning away from the world.

21

Tasha hurtled through Hazel Grove, her dress streaming like a cloak behind her. She could barely see where she was going because her eyes were filled with the awful bloodiness of Zee's face.

'Awch!' She tripped on her high heels, and sprawled full length on the pavement. The long dress ripped and her carefully pinned hair came tumbling down.

Home, she thought, picking herself up and rushing on, I must ring an ambulance... the police... must tell them. 'Mum! Mum!'

She crashed in, shoeless, on the dinner party. For a split second everyone stared at her in astonishment, then her mother leapt up so quickly that her chair flew over backwards.

'What's happened, darling? Are you all right?' Her voice caught. 'Miguel, it's that boy!'

Miguel sprang to his feet, wild as a bull.

'No!' gasped Tasha. 'It's not that! Quickly – get Zee an ambulance!' Her hands flew to her mouth. Waves of emotion rocked over her, and she found that she could not speak at all. Her mother folded her into a hug and held her tightly.

'Someone's attacked Zee, Mum. Her face... she's going to be *disfigured*.'

'Oh no! God!' The colour drained from Magda's

cheeks. 'How...why...?'

Miguel dialled 999 and spoke rapidly to the services. 'They say ambulance and police are already coming – we are safe.'

One of the guests got up. 'We'll go if there's nothing we can do? You don't need us in your way.' They left quickly, muttering horrified goodbyes and Miguel ushered them out to their cars.

'I have to go back,' cried Tasha. 'Oh, Mum! I think this might all have been my fault!'

'You're going nowhere – you're too shocked.'

'But Zee...'

'Zee will be getting all the help she needs. Listen, there's the ambulance already.'

'Her face, Mum, her face! What are we going to do?'

'I-I'm not sure...'

But Miguel had returned and he squeezed Tasha's shoulder gently. 'When you are calm, we will go and help Sue.'

'Sue?'

'Yes. Always we must help the people left behind.'

Gary ran like a fugitive down the hill. Hazel Grove had exploded into action as if it were twelve noon instead of midnight. People were pulling jackets on over pyjamas and shouting to each other as they hurried along.

'Zara Proctor? Dear God, no!'

'Not Con O'Keefe, surely?'

'A punishment beating, in our street?'

'Knives? I hope they get the thugs!'

Someone Gary could not even see stumbled along behind blankets and a pillow. Old Mr Cummings stood in his doorway, the hall light illuminating banked lupins in his garden.

'What have you been up to?' he shouted excitedly as Gary passed the gate and he raised a shaky fist.

'That's my sister!' cried Gary. 'It was nothing to do with me.'

'Neither was thon graffiti I suppose,' huffed Mrs MacGuinness, hurrying past. 'Or that black eye Conor had last week.'

'Think what you want!' he shouted after her. She had him tried and judged already; they all did.

Disappear, Conor had said, stay disappeared.

Gary's brain was pounding. The twins, he remembered, were still alone. They'd be terrified by now. He ran for home but his mother's red Citroën nosed round the bottom corner when he was still fifty yards away.

Instinctively he ducked into the wood. The flashing blue lights of the ambulance swept past him. What on earth would he say to his mother? How could he face her? Neighbours followed close behind her as the car swung into the drive. Then, through the darkness, came a wail he had only heard once before.

The night his dad was murdered.

Blood had splattered up the wall that night, up to the very top, right up above the cornice to the white ceiling with its swirly pattern. Bullets had shattered the glass on a picture of Friesian cattle that hung there. The painting had skewed sideways but not fallen off completely.

Gary, shoeless, had realised slowly that his feet were wet and when he looked down his white socks were red between the toes. Blood was soaking up from the carpet. He was standing in his father's blood. At that moment Gary realised that his dad was dead. But his mum didn't realise. She didn't seem to understand at all and he hadn't known how to make her. She pulled his father close and kissed him, whispered to him, shouted at him to wake up. Her voice had gone on and on until, in the end, she had wailed. Just like this.

Gary vomited. He left the woods and found himself confronted by Conor's father.

'You hanging around my house now? What is it? Is beating up my son not enough for you? Got us lined up for a petrol bomb too, have you?' He pushed him hard.

'I've done nothing!' said Gary stumbling backward. But even he didn't believe that. Whatever he said to Mr O'Keefe, or Mrs MacGuinness or Mr Cummings, or to any of them, he *had* given Des the nod.

Mr O'Keefe wagged his finger in Gary's face. 'The police know all about you – aye they do! I've already told them you've been terrorising our Conor.'

'It wasn't like that!'

'Save it for court, scum! I hope they throw away the key.'

Gary went straight to the Gordons'. He slipped round the back and rapped on the heavy door. There was no answer.

'Get down here,' he shouted. 'Show your face, Des!'

He kept knocking, rattling the handle and shouting. When Des eventually answered he sounded so close that Gary knew he was standing just behind the door.

'Quit yelling!' Des muttered. 'Someone'll hear you. Get out of here before the police come.'

'Des – they've done Zee in – they've slashed her face – she's half dead!' Des said nothing. 'I can't go home, Des, and the place is crawling. Open up and let me in.'

'Go away!' Des shouted.

Questions began to click in Gary's head. He gave the door a kick. 'What do you mean, go away? Open up!'

Why was Des not surprised that Zee was hurt? Why would he not let him in? Why was Des so scared?

'You *knew*,' breathed Gary in disbelief. 'You *knew* it was Zee tonight, didn't you?'

'I was at the window just now,' blurted Des, 'I heard the noise, heard them all talking.'

'Liar!'

From inside came the sound of furniture being dragged across the room. Des was building a barricade and that was as much proof as Gary needed. 'You knew Zee was going with Conor... and you were jealous! You set Zee up!'

'She was going with a Fenian, the wee whore! She needed a slap.'

'She could *die*, Des.'

'That's not my fault – it's Ben's. He's a mad bastard.'

Gary went for the door again, kicking it wildly in frustration, leaving dents in the wood. Then, when the first flash of temper subsided, he called out a warning.

'You won't get away with this, Des Gordon – I'll tell everything.'

'Yeah? It's your word against mine, Gary – I'll deny it all. And who's been in trouble lately? Not me!'

Gary set about kicking down the door, aiming blows at the lock, methodically, over and over again. Eventually it had to give.

Behind him, a voice said quietly, 'Stop doing that right now, Gary.'

It was Mrs Gordon and Gary had no idea how long she'd been there.

'Don't let him in, Ma!' yelled Des, his voice panicky. 'Don't open the door.'

'Des and I need to sort things out,' panted Gary.

'Don't let him in, Ma!'

'The police are looking for you, Gary Proctor,' she said.

'It's not me they want! It's *your* son!'

Des was still babbling on the other side of the door. 'Pity you screwed up your alibi, Gary, 'cos mine's perfect! I've been keeping me old girl company all night, isn't that right, Ma?'

Gary stared at Mrs Gordon and as she stared back he saw her mask slip. For one moment she was not the formidable Mrs G everyone knew. There was someone else there, another version, like a Russian doll, smaller and more vulnerable. In that moment Gary knew that she understood.

'I'll do you a favour,' he said softly. 'I'll make sure Des never bothers either of us again.'

'Don't listen to him, Ma! He's a lyin' toe-rag! Don't you believe a word!'

Mrs Gordon understood him perfectly. Her hand slid almost involuntarily into her coat pocket and Gary heard her keys jingle. He held her eyes for just a second longer, then she shuddered and looked away. The old drawbridge slammed down across her face again.

'You'd better go,' she whispered. 'You're trespassing.'

22

Gary walked quickly. Along the Kensington Road, into Shandon Park, then across the golf course and onto playing fields. Surely panda cars wouldn't follow him across the neatly cut turf. He skirted his old school, one he had attended in another life, it seemed, when he had worn a uniform and sung hymns in assembly.

He made for the Bloomfield Walkway, then weaved expertly through the backstreets of East Belfast. Ruby's territory. For two years he had felt more at home with her family than with his own, but now even Ruby had given up on him. He carried on across the Newtownards Road, the Albert Bridge and Woodstock Links, walking, walking, head down, hands in pockets, past drunks and couples and party-goers.

One o'clock on Sunday morning and Belfast still buzzed. Laughter and teasing spilt from every doorway and crowds thronged the streets determined to enjoy themselves. The politicians kept saying the war was over, but no one really believed them. They knew that the beatings and knee-cappings dished out by para-militaries could explode into full blown war again any time the hard men chose.

A pub with a late licence emptied onto the pavement around him. People hailed taxis, or made for late food stops. The girls had bright hair and careful make-up. Zee a few hours ago, he thought. She had been preening herself in the bathroom mirror tonight. How would she ever look in a mirror again? A chip of ice seemed to turn in his stomach. Hopelessly, for the fiftieth time, he searched his pockets for money.

'Spare us something?' he blurted. Gary had never begged in his life but here he was walking backwards in front of a couple with his hand outstretched. 'Twenty pence for the phone, please?'

'Missed your lift?' scoffed the bloke. 'Try walking.'

'I need to phone the hospital – my sister's ill.'

'Pull the other one.'

But the woman opened her purse.

It took Gary ages to find an empty phone box and get the number from directory enquiries, then, after all that effort, the hospital told him nothing.

'Comfortable,' the voice at the other end said.

'Comfortable?' he repeated. *Comfortable*? How could Zee be comfortable with her face in shreds? Rage took hold of him, his shoulders shook with it, he felt like ripping out the phone cord. But he didn't, he sunk down to the floor with his head in his hands. Only when a girl banged on the door, did he start walking again, watching folk, wondering what to do.

About half past two the crowds thinned and a breeze got up. He walked the railings of the Botanic Gardens until he reached the big ornate gates, then he hauled himself over and made for an old sports pavilion. At least it would shelter him from the wind and the canopy would keep off any drizzle.

He curled up in a corner and stared into the darkness. The city was still not quiet. There was still the odd shout now and then, laughter, an accelerating car. Gary had never felt so alone.

His mother would be with Zee now, at least that was a comforting thought. The pair of them together in the warmth, the ward darkened and hushed. Zee's face cleaned and stitched. *Stitched.* Sweet Jesus, how many stitches?

Who was looking after the twins? Were their temperatures down? God forgive him for running out on them all but what else could he do with the police after him and Conor warning him off...

The wind prowled like a burglar in the bushes, tumbling shadows across the grass, scooping up papers and twigs, and rattling a loose plank in the pavilion wall. It was too spooky to let him sleep, or so he thought until he was jerked awake by Zee's scream and her mauled face swaying like a slashed puppet in his hands.

Gary stumbled up, stiff with cold. The scream he had dreamed had been a real scream he realised; he could still taste it in his throat. He stared suspiciously at the trees and bushes, imagining shapes and movements that were not there. This park could be full of weirdos and druggies who would do him in before they realised that all he possessed were his clothes.

He couldn't stop shivering. The dream had spooked him even more than the park. In his dream Zee's eyes had been blind caves, blood had guttered down her face. He couldn't stop seeing that face even though he was wide awake. Blind caves instead of the contempt he was used to in her eyes.

When their dad died Zee had seemed so shallow; she had barely seemed to care. She had been the first one to cross the doorstep afterwards; she had gone out to buy milk, he remembered. She was the first to eat a meal, to watch a whole film on television, to whistle. Zee had done all the Firsts while he had shrunk down inside himself, hating everyone.

But perhaps he had been wrong and she had cared just as much in her own way. Maybe she had simply made more effort? Behind her no-nonsense, let's-get-on-with-it style, maybe she had been hurting just as much as him. Because tonight, when she clung to him, he had heard something in her voice. When she screamed at him not to leave her he had heard her fear raked up, as raw and permanent as his own. The same feelings, the same fear. People didn't get over things, thought Gary, they just gathered them up, like moss.

A town clock struck five and a lorry revved along the embankment, then came the rattle of a milk float. In the grey pre-light of dawn he heard voices and, peering around the pavilion, he saw two policemen walking towards him.

Gary took off. He ran as fast as his stiff limbs would let him and realised too late that he should have bluffed it out, they were probably just coppers on the beat. When they shouted he panicked and tried to run faster. He glanced behind him and saw one of them speaking into a radio. It seemed a long long way to the railings

211

and he was panting by the time he got there. He threw himself clumsily at the fence, clambered up and slipped and slithered over the spiky top.

Lights swerved down the street and he just knew it was a patrol car. He dropped to the pavement, rolled over and sprang up again, ready to run.

A policeman leapt out of the car before it had stopped. 'What are you up to?' he called.

'Nothing!'

'Is that so?' He grasped Gary firmly by the arm. 'Then you can explain why you were running away.'

At roughly the same time, Tasha was waking up in an armchair in Gary's living room. She stretched stiffly, and her mother, who had been sitting quietly by the fire, smiled at her.

'Okay, love?'

'Mmm. How are Josh and Gemma?'

'Asleep. Thank goodness you were here, I'm not sure they'd have settled for Miguel and me.'

'Has Sue rung from the hospital?'

'No, not for ages.'

Miguel came into the room with a tray of milky drinks but Tasha was too worried to drink hers. She tried, not very successfully, to shield her face behind one hand. If only she could stop feeling guilty.

'Tasha,' said her mum quietly. 'Do you want to talk?'

It took a long time for Tasha to answer and when she did she said, 'I've wanted to talk for ages.'

'Why didn't you, darling?'

She nodded towards Miguel and said, rather apologetically, 'Because of him.' Miguel got up to leave, she noticed, but her mother pulled him back. 'Do you remember the day the two of you turned up at my school unexpectedly, and took me out to tea?'

'Yes, of course I remember.'

'You said you were getting married.'

'We came to ask you to the wedding.'

'Then you went off and did it.'

'At a little registry office in West Ealing.' Her mother was staring hard at her. 'What are you trying to say, Tasha?'

There was a long silence, then Tasha took her courage in both hands. 'You should have asked me if it was okay before you married him.'

'No, I don't agree.'

'You're *my* mum.'

'Which is why I knew how you'd react. I knew you'd be furious. But Miguel's a lovely man, and I knew that, in time, you'd come to see that too.'

'You *knew* an awful lot!' Tasha said fiercely and stared straight ahead into the fire. She wanted to say her piece but if she looked at her mum she would get upset. 'You got it wrong, Mum. It was as if you had *replaced* me.'

'No – never!'

'That's how it felt!'

Her mother put an arm around her. 'Oh, Tasha! Kids are forever.'

'Dream on, Mum!'

'What?' She sounded absolutely flabbergasted.

'Dad doesn't think kids are forever, does he? He's

more a "kids are for when it's convenient" sort of man.'

Her mother gasped. 'You thought I was doing the same thing...how stupid of me! I am sorry. Listen, are you listening to me?'

Tasha nodded.

'I love you more than I love anyone else in the world. I always have done and I always will.'

Tasha glanced at Miguel to see how he was taking this piece of news but Miguel was smiling at her.

'I quite likes you too...' he said, '...sometimes.'

She spluttered with laughter, she couldn't help it; she had been so horrible to Miguel. Her mum pulled all three of them into a hug and for some reason it felt almost okay. It occurred to Tasha that however much she had felt alone during the last six months, she had never actually been alone. Her mum had been here all the time, waiting for her to come back.

Miguel cleared his throat. 'Now, this terrible thing tonight – you said earlier is your fault. Why do you think so?'

'Do you remember the day of the party, Miguel, when Gary was jealous of Conor? He's still jealous. I think it was Gary who set things up tonight – he was trying to hurt Conor. He thought it was *me* going out with Conor, not Zee. You see, I told him so the night of the garden party just to keep him off my back.'

'Pah! This does not make it your fault. It is the fault of evil men. It is the same always – they make you blame yourself.'

Tasha was not sure what he was talking about,

something from his past, perhaps, but it made her feel a little better.

'Why don't you ring the hospital?' her mum suggested. 'See if there's any more news?'

Tasha nodded. Perhaps it was time she pulled herself together.

It was dark when Zee woke up. She knew, without looking around, that she was in hospital, knew it without taking in the grey single room, or the oxygen mask poised above her bed. She knew it because she remembered every awful detail. In disaster movies, people wake up blissfully unaware, then their memories leach slowly back. Real life was different, Zee already knew that because she had learned it when her dad died. Each morning, she had woken up hurting, the truth turning like a jagged splinter inside her. Awake or asleep, in real life there was no escape from horror.

Beside her, in a chair, her mother snored gently. Zee was relieved because just for a few minutes she wanted to be on her own. She moved her head slowly and it wasn't too painful after all. It just felt strange, her face tight and swollen, like an oven-ready chicken, too tightly trussed. Not like her real face at all.

She raised one hand and touched her cheek. It felt odd somehow, waxy. She touched a wound and let her finger follow a winding row of stitches that ran almost from chin to nose. A panicky whimper rose up inside her but she didn't let it out. She took a deep breath and kept going. Up a bit, she found another row of stitches. Then another. Her fingers began to shake. They trembled across four rows of stitches with poking-out jagged ends. Zee raised her other hand, open palmed, and her other cheek felt just as bad. Something like a volcano began to erupt inside her and from the inside out, her body began to shake. Shock hit her like a bus.

'It's okay!' Instantly awake, her mother flung her arms around her. 'You're safe now, d'you hear? Safe.'

Tears flooded Zee's cheeks, only they didn't flood downward, not like they were meant to. Diverted by dykes of stitches they trickled off her cheeks, around her ears, down her neck and under the starched hospital gown she was wearing. Her very own tears frightened her terribly. They ran on for ages, getting into all sorts of places they wouldn't usually, wetter, wilder, more out of control than tears had ever been.

'What's wrong, what's wrong?' she gasped, and her mum, not understanding, began to talk about the night before.

'It was awful,' Zee interrupted. 'You can't imagine ... I was so terrified.'

'I know, I've been imagining it all night ...'

'He was horrible, Mum, *horrible*.'

'Oh, love.'

'I'll be scarred for life.'

'Not ... necessarily. The doctor says it's too early to tell. And ... there's always plastic surgery.'

Another huge sob escaped Zee. It could take years for surgeons to reconstruct a face. She'd seen programmes about it. What about the meantime? Little kids in shopping malls would stare at her. The girls at school would try hard not to stare. They'd talk to her with their perfect faces, they'd be extra nice... she couldn't bear it.

And the boys... no boy would ever come near her again. As for Con... another sob broke loose. Why had she ever got involved with Conor?

'Whatever happens,' said her mum grittily, 'I'm here for you. Always, forever. You do know that, don't you?'

More sobs rumbled through Zee's body. How many scarred foreign correspondents had she seen on telly? Her career was in tatters before it started.

'We'll get through this, Zee. We've coped in the past and we'll cope now. We're all behind you. Conor will be in to see you as soon as he wakes up.'

'No!'

'But—'

'Is he here? In the hospital?'

'He went home a couple of hours ago. He's had a beating but they didn't touch him with the knife.'

'I don't want him coming near me, Mum.'

'But he's worried sick, he's coming back this afternoon.'

'Not like this – no!'

Her mother looked flustered. 'Look, can I get you anything?' she asked. 'A drink, perhaps?'

'There is one thing.'

'*Anything*.'

'A mirror.'

She saw her mother swallow hard. Emotion swelled

Sue's face and her eyes glistened.

'No, love,' she whispered.

'But you said anything, you promised me.'

'There'll be plenty of time later.'

'I want one now.'

'*No*.'

'It's my face – *mine*. I want to *see* it. Let me see!' She was crying again, but with fury this time.

Her mother had rushed to the door. 'Nurse, nurse! She's getting upset.'

Zee knew that she was shouting, she knew she should stop, but part of her just didn't want to.

'What's all this?' demanded a nurse with sledge-hammer arms.

'I want a mirror!'

'Don't be silly, dear. Calm down.'

Silly? That made Zee wilder still. She started thrashing about even though it made her face hurt. There was a bit of a tussle, some shouting, mostly from her, then an undignified pinprick in the bum. As if being knifed wasn't enough, now they were sticking needles in her. Zee glimpsed darkness beyond the window then it came swirling quickly in and swallowed her up completely.

23

Gary's dad had always told him not to believe in TV cops but of course he had. Car chases with flashing lights and screaming sirens, villains spread-eagled against walls, stark interview rooms featuring Detectives Nasty and Nice. Why else would anyone join the police force for heaven's sake?

But maybe, Gary thought now, maybe his dad had been right because so far things had been okay. The room they were in had a bubbling coffee machine, a big leafy plant and pictures on the walls. Earlier, this Sergeant Carson had rung the hospital for him and told him that Zee was out of danger. He'd even produced coffee and a sandwich. Weirdest of all, the Sergeant seemed to be saying that he wasn't to blame.

'But I am,' said Gary impatiently, 'I've explained it. What happened to Zee was *my* fault too.'

'Mrs Gordon says differently.'

Gary blinked in surprise. 'Mrs G? Is she here?'

'She was last night. She turned her boy in. Des came clean eventually and confessed to everything.'

Gary could hardly believe it. So Mrs G had overheard them talking last night after all. She had not wanted him to tear Des limb from limb, but she had recognised the truth all right.

'I can't believe she'd grass up her own flesh and

blood,' he muttered.

'If more people informed then peace would stand a better chance,' said the Sergeant crisply. 'The real thugs would be caught, there'd be fewer punishment beatings. Maybe your sister wouldn't be lying in hospital right now with her face slashed.'

Gary couldn't look him in the eyes.

'Is there anything you want to tell me, Gary?'

'No.' His voice sounded unconvincingly small. Sergeant Carson didn't say a word. He was waiting for Gary to change his mind. 'No,' Gary repeated, too loudly this time.

'Right then, let's talk about your mate, Des.'

'Some mate.'

'What did Jack think of Des?'

'Jack, my dad?' Gary was astonished. 'Did you know my dad?'

'Certainly I did, we trained together. He was a good bloke. I can't think Jack would have wanted you and Des to be best mates.'

'We weren't always. Dad felt sorry for Des though – not having a dad of his own. He used to invite him out with us sometimes – to the cinema, McDonald's, places like that.'

'Go on.'

'When Dad died – got murdered – Des stuck by me. Some of me other mates didn't know where to look, what to say. Some of them went outa their way to avoid me, but Des was never like that. He hated those murderers just as much as I did. He seemed to know how I felt.'

'Oh?'

'Dad was the best,' said Gary, 'the *very* best and Des thought so too.'

'How d'you mean, Gary?'

'Once, when Dad was giving us a lift, he got called to this robbery. He pulled out his gun, went in, and arrested two men – just like that!' Gary clicked his fingers decisively. 'Des hero-worshipped him after that.'

Sergeant Carson cleared his throat. 'Des's own dad was a toe-rag, you know.'

'So?'

'He walked out of Des's life and never once looked back. Hasn't sent him as much as a birthday card since.'

'What are you saying, Sergeant Carson?'

'How do you think Des feels about you, Gary?'

'I don't know. You mean . . . he's jealous?'

'Of course he's jealous. And not just of your dad. There are other things too – like your reputation with the girls. Des said as much last night, whereas he . . .'

'. . . Can't get a girl interested,' finished Gary. Suddenly it all made some sort of sense. 'Then my sister tells him to get lost and . . .'

'It was more than Des's pride could take. He saw his chance to be top man for once and he took it.'

'He's sick!' shouted Gary. 'How could slashing Zee's face make Des top man?'

'He claims the violence got out of hand, says he only intended Zee to get a slap. He wanted to scare her, bring her to heel.'

'I'll kill him!' vowed Gary. Seized by anger he

banged the table with his fist. 'I swear I'll *kill* him.'

'What good will that do?' said the Sergeant sharply. 'The law will deal with Des now. He'll go to a young offender institute.'

Gary raked his hands through his hair and tried to calm himself. It didn't seem right to ask the next question but he had to know the answer. 'What about me, Sergeant Carson? What's going to happen to me?'

'You paid no one, Gary, stole nothing, made none of the arrangements. Des would have gone ahead with or without you. It was just easier to string you along, and a bit of a power trip for Des.'

It took a moment for this to hit home. 'You mean... I'm free to go?'

'We'd rather you stayed – to help us with our enquiries.'

The phrase echoed round Gary's head. He'd heard it so many time on telly but now it was for real. A thin sweat broke out on his top lip, he knew it must be glistening. 'I can't help you,' he blurted out. 'I know nothing.'

The Sergeant stared at him, just stared, then he said, 'I don't believe you. I thought you'd want to help your sister, Gary.'

'Of course I do. If I could turn back the clock, don't you think I would?'

'You can't. But there is one thing you can do to help her.' He looked Gary grimly in the eyes. 'Des wouldn't tell us the names of the men who attacked Zee – he's too frightened for his own features. But we need their names, Gary, and you know them.'

Gary shook his head fiercely. 'I don't!'

Sweat started oozing out all over him, like suds squeezed from a scouring pad. Not names, he wanted to shout, anything but names. He tried to find his voice again but it was stuck somewhere deep down inside him. All he could do was stare at his own hands which were damp and twisting and seemed to have taken on a life of their own.

'Zee could meet those two any day,' said the Sergeant, 'just walking around town. Do you want that to happen to her?'

Gary's eyes closed at the very thought of it.

'Think what your help here would mean to her. Think what it would mean to your mother. Don't you think they've been through enough?'

Gary's heart started beating hard, louder and louder, faster and faster, like a train screaming through a tunnel.

'I can't!' he shouted. 'You *know* what they do to grassers – they torture them – they cut bits off them! *Then* they kill them.'

'These two fellas will be in prison quite a time, Gary.'

'But their mates won't. *And* they will get released one day. Hell, if there's another amnesty, maybe next week!'

Sergeant Carson leaned so close that Gary could see the plaque on his teeth. 'Your dad was really proud of you,' he said softly. 'If he could see you now... and Jack was such a brave man too.'

Tears rocketed into Gary's eyes. They shocked him, took him completely by surprise. He buried his face in his hands but there was nowhere to hide in this tiny room, and the policeman just kept on staring.

'You've got a choice, Gary,' he said at last. 'A chance. You can put yourself first and let everyone down – again – or you can do what's right. You can make a difference here, son. Which is it going to be?'

The rattle of a lunch trolley woke Zee. Mince and tatties by the smell of it. Her mum was dozing in the chair again but she jerked awake the moment Zee sat up.

'Do I look as bad as you do?' asked Zee.

'Probably not.' She groaned, stretched, and pushed her straggling pepper and salt hair off her face. 'What is that awful smell?'

'Lunch. You know, Mum, your forehead's got so many wrinkles this morning it looks like a ploughed field.'

'Thanks. I can always depend on my kids to flatter me.'

'I bet it looks better than mine.'

'Don't.' Her tone was gently firm. 'You were sounding so much more like yourself.'

Zee nodded. She certainly felt a whole lot better. The weepiness had gone, and the panic. 'Do you promise not to stick any more needles in me?' she asked.

'Only if you promise not to go ballistic. You kicked a nurse – I've never been so mortified.'

'Did I?' Zee squirmed in the big bed. 'Sorry – I don't know what came over me earlier.'

'It's called reaction.' Her mum grinned and squeezed her hand.

She would probably never mention it again, she was good that way. She didn't harp on – or only about keeping bedrooms tidy – not about things that really mattered. Affection surged through Zee.

'Mum... about me and Con... I'm sorry I didn't tell you earlier. I really wanted to, I *hated* lying. But after the eleventh night, when Gary let rip on the landing next morning, I didn't think you'd let me see Conor. '

'I'm sorry too, love, I should have been braver. I should have encouraged you and Conor, not been afraid how Gary might react.'

'You are brave,' said Zee indignantly. 'These last two years with the twins throwing tantrums... Gary's moods... it's been so... so *different* for each of us, and awful for you too. But you've been there for us all, since Day One.'

'Just being there isn't enough,' said Sue heavily. 'Last night, sitting here, I realised that.'

'What do you mean?' asked Zee as her mum pummelled her pillows into a more comfortable position.

'For the last two years I've been wrapping us up in cotton wool, planting flowers for the future, going to peace vigils – it's not enough, love. I hoped, I *believed* that the politicians would sort things out, but last night I realised it's going to take more than that. We've all got to do our bit.'

She was starting to sound like Conor. 'Which bit are you going to do?' asked Zee bleakly.

Her mother looked determined, in spite of her tiredness. 'I'm going to do that training course and when it's over I'm going to teach in Laggan College.'

'The cross-community school? Gary's not going to

225

like that. Have you told him? What did he say about last night?'

'Gary's disappeared, love. The Molotovs say he hasn't been back.'

Zee stared at the shiny hospital walls and the big glass window that stretched from floor to ceiling.

Gary's voice came echoing back to her. *'Ben, get off her! Leave her be!'*

Then Conor rounding on him. *'You knew their names!'* he had shouted accusingly and Gary hadn't denied it.

'This wasn't meant to happen,' he had said.

Gary was mixed up in it all right and she had sent him away because otherwise Conor would have torn him apart.

Suddenly voices outside the door jerked her back to the present. The twins' voices, high and excited. The door burst open and Zee's hands flew to her face but there was no time and no place to hide.

'What on earth—' began her mother.

Dozens of flowers seemed to lurch crazily into the room, gladioli, roses, carnations, chrysanthemums and a mass of others that Zee could not even begin to name. Magda, Miguel and Tasha smiled at her awkwardly from behind the blooms while out from underneath shot the twins.

'Careful!' squealed their mother. 'Zee's hurt.'

Covered in chicken pox and petals, and with the same gorilla nurse in hot pursuit, the twins hurled themselves onto the bed.

'Sure you're up to this?'

Zee nodded; she was just hugely relieved that it wasn't Conor.

Suddenly the twins stopped dead. They knelt on the bed, staring at her, not saying a word and not daring to touch her.

'Cat got your tongues?' asked their mum.

'It's still me!' Zee tried to sound cheerful but somehow her voice came out desperate instead.

Then, very gravely, Josh said, 'I just hope they gave you the brandy this time.'

Zee started laughing and the rest of them joined in, a little uncertainly at first. They laughed for a full minute. She hugged Josh, much to his disgust, and used the opportunity to wipe her damp eyes on his shirt.

'Visiting is not until two o'clock,' the nurse said crisply, 'after lunch.'

'Sorry,' said Magda humbly. 'We couldn't keep the children away a second longer.'

'They have chicken pox,' thundered the nurse, 'and *this* is a hospital.'

'But it isn't infectious once the spots are up,' said Sue.

Magda smiled at her gratefully. 'You really don't mind us coming?'

'Not at all. I knew they'd be desperate to see Zee. Thanks so much for looking after them last night.'

'Visiting is *after* lunch,' boomed the nurse, 'not before.'

'I don't want lunch,' Zee told her. 'But I would like to see my brother and sister.'

'Five minutes,' said the nurse. 'Not a second longer. I'd better find some vases.'

227

'All these flowers . . . ' began Zee. 'Thank you so much.'

'The neighbours,' said Miguel, 'had a whirl about.'

'He means a whip round,' said Tasha.

Zee gulped back a mixture of laughter and tears. She mustn't get all emotional again. 'Please thank them for me, won't you?'

'Can I count your stitches?' asked Gemma. 'I can count up to a hundred. Will that be high enough?'

'Of course it will,' said her mother spikily.

Josh touched her face. 'What happens if I pull this thread, Zee?'

'I thump you, that's what happens.'

'See?' Sue was smiling with satisfaction. 'It's still our Zee underneath.'

Magda looked at Zee solemnly. 'Miguel and I always thought you were pretty level headed, Zee, but Tasha has told us all about the last few weeks and now I know just how much we have to thank you for.'

'I don't know what you mean,' blurted Zee.

'You've been a brilliant friend to her.'

'I didn't do anything.' Zee blushed, wishing that she could escape somewhere.

'Yes, you did. Tasha told us how you took care of her, introduced her to people, even warned her off Gar – er – boys. You stuck by her. And when she got into . . . difficulties . . . you took her to that clinic.'

Zee stole a glance at her mother whose eyes had narrowed suspiciously but Tasha did not look in the least embarrassed. She was grinning, in fact she was practically boiling over with excitement.

'You'll never guess what,' she said. 'Can I tell her, Mum?'

'Tell me what?'

'Let me explain,' said Magda but it was Sue she turned to, not Zee. 'I've been talking to Tasha's father on the phone. Filling him in. He was horrified to hear about last night, and very relieved that it wasn't Tasha. The thing is . . . he's rather wealthy. He's offered to pay for Zee to go to school with Tasha – at Redbales.'

'Good Lord!'

'What do you think of that, Zee?' Tasha rushed to the bedside and pumped Zee's arm up and down. You'll get loads of new clothes and meet all my friends and in a year or two you'll be right there in Fleet Street! Isn't it *fantastic*?'

Zee was almost speechless. 'Does . . . he mean it?'

'Absolutely,' said Magda.

'We could visit you,' shouted Gemma, catching Tasha's excitement 'We could go to London and watch the changing of those furry guards.'

'But Zee may need plastic surgery,' her mum said suddenly.

'They have surgeons also in London,' said Miguel.

'But the best ones are here in Belfast. They've had lots of practice!'

Magda reached out and touched Sue's arm lightly. 'It's only a suggestion, my dear. But Zee would be safe there.'

'Could Gary visit Zee too?' piped Josh.

The temperature in the little room seemed to drop

229

suddenly. Gemma whispered, not very quietly in her mother's ear, 'Is Gary bad now?'

'No,' she replied loudly. 'He's just confused.'

Everyone seemed to be looking at their feet. If it hadn't all been so horribly embarrassing, it would have been funny, thought Zee.

'Will Gary come home if Zee goes away?' asked Gemma.

Josh picked up a book lying on the locker and hurled it on the floor. 'I want Gary *and* Zee to come home. And Mummy. *And* Daddy.'

'Ssh,' said Sue pulling them both onto her lap and wrapping them up in a cuddle. Zee could tell that she was close to tears.

'Mum, you're exhausted. Please go home with the twins. They need you and you need some proper sleep, and I . . . I need to think.'

Tasha's face crashed. 'You will come to Redbales, won't you?'

'I'll think about it. But you have to do something for me, Tasha.'

'Of course . . . anything.'

'Right, then. Find Gary.'

'Oh, Zee!'

'He must be desperate, Tasha. He didn't mean to hurt me – I'm sure of it. I need to see Gary before I go anywhere. I can't leave things like this.'

Tasha nibbled her lower lip but Miguel put his arm around her shoulders and said, 'Would you like me to help you?'

'Yes, I would like that.' Tasha looked up at him with a smile as wide as the world.

How beautiful she is, thought Zee, then she recalled how alike people had said they were, and something started choking her deep inside. 'I think I'd like to sleep now,' she told them.

'Good.' Her mother kissed her. 'Later, the police want to talk to you.'

'Okay.'

'And about Conor, love . . . '

'Keep him away, Mum.'

'But he's so keen to see you.'

'No! There's only one guy I want to see – Gary.'

24

Tasha's first stop was with Des. She detested him; he was the most vulgar lout she had ever met. But she had promised Zee that she would do everything possible to find Gary, and if that meant screwing up her courage to ask Des, then that was what she would do.

It was Mrs Gordon who answered the door, not Des. She was wearing a pink nylon housecoat and she held a long-handled feather-duster in her hand like a sword. She told Tasha that the police had charged Des. He would not be back for a long time apparently and she intended to advertise for a lodger. She was busy turning out his room, she said, and could not stop to chat. Tasha turned away from the door without having spoken a word.

Together, she and Miguel combed Hazel Grove. They searched the wood and crossed the paving slabs where Tasha and Zee had tipsily played hopscotch. Tasha asked the boys playing football behind the Co-op if they had seen Gary but they shook their heads. Tasha had been avoiding the football pitch for weeks but now she stared at the patch of grass where she had lost her virginity, and somehow, it didn't seem that important any more. Like the boys playing football, all she could manage was a shrug.

Later she and Miguel scoured the streets, looked into local shops and rang Sue twice. There was still no sign of Gary.

'We'll get the car,' said Miguel, 'and search in the city.'

They cruised the streets then drove into the centre of town, stopping to look in cheap cafés and amusement arcades. Miguel scoured the pubs and he talked encouragingly to Tasha when she felt hopeless. 'It will take time but at least he is alive. We *will* find him.'

Back home Magda told them she had rung the police. Apparently Gary had been questioned and then released. One more call to Sue, then darkness had descended.

'You must stop, you both look exhausted. I've made a cottage pie for supper.'

They ate it hungrily, followed by an apple crumble. 'Tomorrow, Miguel, will you help me search again?' asked Tasha.

'Of course, and every day until we find him.'

Tasha was suddenly and unexpectedly happy.

At three o'clock that afternoon Gary had left Shaftesbury Square police station. Around him the pigeons were making a huge racket. With chests puffed out, they were perched like the beads of a necklace, all along the window ledges of Victorian office blocks, cackling at the traffic below. It was jammed solid. Irate drivers blared their horns, exhausts belched fumes, litter catapulted along dusty gutters.

Why were they all in such a hurry, Gary wondered. What mattered so much? He wandered aimlessly down to the city centre, his hands in his empty pockets. Go home, Sergeant Carson had told him but Gary had no intention of doing that. He had done too much harm there already. Zee would never want to see him again and they would all be better off without him.

In front of the City Hall he stretched out on the wilting summer grass and let the sun work like a masseur on his bones, warming and soothing them. Exhausted, he would have slept, but a knot of fear in his stomach tightened and jerked him awake every time he dozed off.

Had Jimmy and Ben been picked up yet, he wondered. Was he safe here in the middle of city crowds? Would he ever be safe again?

When the town clock struck five Gary hauled himself up and began walking east towards the hospital. Perhaps, if he went there in person, they would tell him more. He avoided the backstreets he had come to know so well, sticking instead to the main roads where Belfast's red double-deckers ploughed up and down in a haze of diesel.

The traffic eased after six and the sun descended in a dirty silver disc into city smog. A few punters lingered outside pubs, pints in hand, winding down after work. For the first time ever, Gary envied them their hard day's work and their well-deserved drinks.

Salt and vinegar smells prickled his nostrils when he passed a corner chippy and from a pizza hut wafted the musky aroma of Italian herbs. His stomach gurgled with hunger. By seven o'clock he was glancing into the metal council bins screwed onto lamp-posts. But he would not sink that low, not as low as the drop-outs and rough sleepers he had seen scavenging before now, and despised. Not until darkness came anyway, when the sight of a half-eaten fish supper was too much to resist.

Outside the Ulster Hospital he stood for a long time looking up at the tower block of brightly lit windows. Which room was Zee's? Was she up there staring down at him? Or was she too ill to get out of bed? Had she had surgery? Or even relapsed into unconsciousness again?

He prowled like a thief around the car park until he had satisfied himself that his mother's red Citroën was not there. Someone must have persuaded her to go home. That had to be a good sign because she would never leave if Zee was critical. Gary plucked up his courage and sidled into reception.

A girl with candy floss hair asked for Zee's details and her pink fingernails tapped them into a keyboard as he spoke.

'Which ward, lovee?'

'Um I dunno – er – facial wounds.'

'Pardon?'

Gary couldn't bring himself to say it again. All he really wanted to do was bolt. 'Zara Proctor – she was brought into accident and emergency, last night.'

'Are you a relative?'

'Yeah – a cousin.'

Her eyes never left the monitor. 'Right, I've got her – she's in ward seven.'

'What else?' he asked.

'Nothing else,' she said blankly. 'If you go up they might just give you a few minutes but visiting's over really.'

'I don't want to go up,' he said awkwardly, 'I just want to know how she's getting on.'

The girl swivelled round in her seat, her huge mascaraed eyes settling on him like sun lamps. 'This is just a database,' she said as if he was too stupid to realise that. 'We don't hold information about the patients' health here.'

'Someone must be able to tell me something.'

She looked him up and down. 'Well...if you want to take a seat, I'll ask the duty doctor if he'll see you.'

'Don't bother.' A doctor might tell Zee that he was here and frighten the life out of her. 'Can't you find out if she's had plastic surgery? Is she in tears all the time? How *is* she?'

'Sorry, you really do need to talk to a doctor, lovee.'

If this bimbo called him lovee one more time he'd hit her. Gary walked across the foyer and leaned against a pillar. Emotion rolled like boulders across his chest and he had to fight hard to control it.

'Are y'all right there?' said a voice. 'Ye look shockin' so you do.'

Gary would have known that voice anywhere. He stared at her dumbfounded.

'Hello, ye pillock!'

'Ruby...what are you doing here?'

'Waitin' for a heart transplant.' She scowled at him. 'What d'ye think I'm doin'? I'm waitin' for ye of course.'

'You said we were finished,' he reminded her.

'And ye said there's far too much between us. Ye're right.'

236

Her hair looked rattier than ever and there was more metal in her face than in the shipyard but at that precise moment, there was no one in the whole world Gary would rather have seen.

'I knew ye'd come here eventually,' she said gruffly, 'but ye didn't half take yer time! Know how many flamin' *National Geographics* I've had to read?'

Gary buried his head between her breasts and smelt that amazing mixture of patchouli and nicotine and chips that was pure Ruby.

'Oh, Jeezus, Ruby, what the hell am I going to do?' he asked.

'What d'ye think, y'eejit?' She kissed the back of his neck like his mum used to when he was a little boy. 'You're gonna come home wi' me.'

25

Just a few hundred yards down the hospital corridor, Conor paused. He had wanted to be a surgeon for two years now but tonight this hospital was spooking him. Everything was so quiet and orderly on the surface, but somewhere here cancer patients must be sucking in their final breaths, crash victims would be hurtling towards theatre. Conor had imagined himself as a skilled, hard-working doctor putting the grateful injured back together again. He had never thought about patients feeling angry, like Sue said Zee felt. There were so many people here with their lives in chaos and his own girlfriend was one of them.

In the lift his hands slid nervously around the control panel before he found the right button to press, and on the fourth floor he took a deep breath to steady himself before walking self-consciously along the corridor. Sue's message rang in his ears. *Stay away, Conor. Give her time.*

His stomach began to flutter. He wondered if he ought to peer through the little window in her door first, get a look at her, prepare himself. But a nurse might notice him doing that and stop him visiting altogether. In the end he marched straight in.

'Get out!' she screamed, disappearing under the duvet. All Conor glimpsed was the top of her head. At least that looked normal.

'Thanks,' he said jerkily, 'lovely welcome.'

'I *told* you to stay away.'

'I couldn't – sorry – I had to come.'

From under the duvet came a furious cry. 'I don't *want* you here, Conor.'

'Why not? Why won't you see me?'

'Why do you think?'

Conor tried hard to be kind. 'I don't care how you look, you know.'

'Bully for you, Conor! I mind.' A strangled sob escaped her.

'Of course you do! I know that, *I know*.'

He flopped down on a chair, feeling useless, and wishing that he had planned what to say, but the truth was he had no idea. What words could possibly put this right? Besides, Zee had always been the one with the words. They sat in silence, separated by a stupid sheet of cotton.

'What did your dad say?' she asked at last.

That threw him, but at least she was speaking. 'Um . . . he called Gary all sorts of words you don't find in the dictionary. Then he did the same to Des.'

'And to me too, I suppose?'

'No, not at all. They've been worried about you – we all have.'

Her voice softened a little. 'Did they give you a hard time? For seeing me behind their backs?'

'Actually they've been great these last few days.' He was quiet for a moment, thinking just how supportive they had been. 'It's as if they finally understand that my life's my own – and it's going to be different to theirs.'

The sheet sagged just then, enough for him to see her eyebrows and one wound. Fleshiness, juicily red, bulged between the stitches. He swallowed quickly.

'Has Gary come home yet?' she asked.

'I dunno.' Anger swelled inside him. 'I don't suppose the prodigal son will come knocking on my door though, I might just tear his head off.'

'You will not! This was Des's fault, not Gary's. Des saw me at the window that night. It was Des behind this – I know it was.'

Conor could hardly believe what he was hearing. 'Gary was involved – you know that! None of this would have happened if Gary hadn't been hellbent on keeping us apart, Zee.'

'You know how screwed up Gary is.'

Was she really going to let him off the hook that easily? Conor struggled to keep his voice calm. 'Gary's still responsible for what he does, Zee.'

'I know, but Des *used* him, and he is still my brother.'

Bitterness broke like a wave through Conor's voice. 'Gary's finally going to get what he wants. He really *is* going to separate us this time, isn't he?'

'You mean ... Mum's told you I'm going to England?'

'She's told me you're thinking about it. She came round to the house and the four of us sat in our front room drinking tea out of the best china. It felt like someone had died, Zee. But you *haven't* died, and I don't want you going away.'

'It'll be for the best,' she said.

'How can it be? I *love* you.'

'You won't, Conor – not now. Nobody could.'

'*I* will . . . of course I will . . . Zee, show me . . . *please.*'

Slowly she lowered the duvet.

Shock hit him like an earthquake; he could no more keep it out of his face than he could turn away. Disfigured, destroyed, her beautiful face gone. How could they do that to her? How could anyone destroy a person's face? It was like stealing a whole life away. Conor could neither move nor speak but she was staring at him, waiting. She was watching him watching her.

'God,' he said, his voice as dry as salt. 'Oh my God . . .'

'It's bad, isn't it?' she whispered. 'They won't give me a mirror. Tell me, Conor, *how* bad?'

His answer mattered, he knew that, but she looked as if her face was covered in spaghetti and blotched with Bolognese. Words sat like hurdles in his throat and he had to force each one out separately. 'You're still beautiful to me,' he said.

'*Liar!*'

She burst into tears and threw herself down on the mattress. Conor hurried round the bed and knelt on the floor beside her. 'It's not too bad, not once you get used to it. There's one big wound under your eye. The rest . . . they . . . they don't look too deep. They'll mebbe heal up and you'll get your looks back . . . maybe.'

'You don't look so hot yourself, Romeo!'

That was more like Zee. He smiled with relief and touched his bruised eye. 'This is a corker, isn't it? I've three stitches in my lip and broken ribs too.'

241

'But yours *will* heal, Conor. You *will* be okay.'

'And yours might. Whether they do, or whether they don't, I'll still love you, Zee.'

She let slip a huge sob, but when he reached out to comfort her, she shrank away.

'Don't! I want to go away, Conor, I *want* to go to England. Tasha's dad is giving me a future.'

'You've a future here. I told my parents I love you. I even told the police. I've hardly slept since Saturday, I can't eat, I can't concentrate. Zee, we have a future together.' She didn't answer, she didn't say anything at all and suddenly he felt completely powerless. 'You can't let this beat you, Zee!'

'I can.'

'Do you really want to break up? After all we've been through? All this for nothing?'

'All this? What am I, Con, some cross-community project?' She had a tongue like a whip sometimes. 'Maybe that's all I've ever been to you.'

'Don't talk rubbish.'

'There are lots of nice Catholic girls in Belfast. Do yourself a favour and find one.'

'You don't mean that.'

'I do. Northern Ireland's never going to change. I've had it – I'm leaving here and I'm *never* coming back.'

'You're just scared, more scared than ever – I'll help you, I promise I will.'

She reached for a cord above the bed and pressed the buzzer on the end of it. 'I don't want your help, you arrogant git – get out!'

242

Tears ricocheted between her wounds like a game of pinball. Conor watched in horror. He had come here to make her feel better but instead he had made her worse. He had made her cry. He had made her face come alive with repulsive wriggling worms. All these fine words he'd spouted, but if she did stay, would he really be able to love her?

'Out,' she yelled again and a nurse appeared at the same time. 'Out!'

'Okay... but I'll be back.'

Would he? Did he really want her? Did he even want to be a surgeon after seeing this? The world was shifting under his feet and nothing seemed certain any more. Overcome with confusion, he backed away. It felt as if some long road was unravelling between them, pushing them further and further apart. Down the length of it their eyes met and in that moment he saw that Zee was letting him go. He fought it for a moment then he turned and walked away.

A blade came glinting towards her again... those eyes glittering through jagged holes. The stench of him... sweat and beer and stale breath... she heard herself beg for mercy.

'No... no... please don't!'

The sound of her own voice woke her up as it often did now. Zee propped herself up on one arm and drank from the glass on her bedside locker. It rattled a little against her teeth and when she rolled back onto the mattress her nightdress was clammy with sweat.

Perhaps she should ask them for another of those little blue tablets to calm her down.

She slipped shakily out of bed and walked slowly to the ensuite lavatory. Going to the loo still felt like an adventure. She had only been allowed up a few times, though this evening – Tuesday she thought – they had even let her have a bath.

She washed her hands, frowning at a square of bright paint above the basin. She had noticed it before, it looked odd, as if something had been removed. Suddenly she realised what should have been there. They had taken away the mirror.

Did she really look so awful? Did they think she would die of a heart attack if she saw her own reflection? She hung onto the basin, steadying herself. Perhaps she should go and find a nurse and demand a mirror.

But they wouldn't listen to her. They would just call her an hysterical kid again, they might even give her another jab. Besides, she had no energy for a scene. How could she feel so tired, she wondered, when all she had done for days was lie in bed? The heat in the little room was stifling. Perhaps she could open a window and let in a blast of cool night air.

Nighttime, the window would be black. Zee's heart leapt. She would be able to see her reflection in the darkened window.

In a few steps she had crossed the room. She hesitated for a second, then fixed her eyes on the floor, concentrating on one particular tile. Keeping her sights pinned there, she pulled the string that gathered back the curtains. Wait . . . wait . . . she had to be ready for this.

She looked up and her breath rushed out with a cry. Another breath now, a longer one. She held it, let it go. After that it was easier to breathe and look at the same time.

It is me. Zee. Underneath that . . . mess . . . it's me.

In the window she saw her tongue slide between her lips, moistening them; suddenly they were parched.

'One . . . two . . . three . . . ' She began to count the wounds, just as Gemma had. Stay logical, get a handle on it, count. Breathing hard, she went on. One big blotch beneath the eye, just like Conor had said.

That was when the man had wrenched the knife round, twisting it in, pushing hard, like a knife into a peach. But it was her own flesh, no peach, that had flicked down bloodily around her. It had hurt so much. She gulped for breath as the memories tightened like a plastic bag around her mouth. His arm, thick as a branch, pinning her down, but worse than that, much worse, the smell of her own blood, warm and sticky. It had buckled her legs in terror. She remembered – like a lightning streak – where she had smelt blood just like it once before.

Her father's blood. Smelt it, seen it. Bright arterial red, still frothing, running down the wallpaper, splattered over furniture. The metallic warmth of it cloying at her nostrils. The deep pile of the carpet bunching as the dark stain spread.

Fear had cut her off from everyone that night, it had bandaged her tight as an Egyptian mummy, had separated her off from Gary and her mother. She remembered being unable to speak, remembered turning and leaving them there together among the blood. She had taken Josh into bed with Gemma and lain there listening to the sirens wail while the twins slept peacefully on either side of her. In the morning, while Sue dozed and Gary raged, Zee had made them toast. For months she had managed to forget, but not now.

'*This is for your da*,' that man had said.

Her dad? Why had her dad left them all alone? How dare he? Please come back, Dad. A crushing pain worse than any physical one gripped her. She screwed up her eyes hard. When she opened them again and looked in the window, there was another face beside hers.

'Dad!' She spun round but the room was empty and when she turned back to the window he had gone. 'Dad!'

But she had seen him, she *had*, right there in the window beside her. She twisted back and forth but there was no sign of him, now, not in the room, not in the window. Only her own smashed face, half-stranger, staring back.

Was it a ghost? Or a memory that had jumped out unasked? She crawled into bed, scared of the memories she kept packed away somewhere deep inside her. It upset her to talk about her dad. It upset her when Gary and Sue did.

But the memories leaked out now and she couldn't stop them. His funeral had been so awful. They had draped his coffin in a Union Jack – as if that made a difference – and lowered him, lurching slightly, into a deep slit in the ground. Sue had screamed as they took him, finally, away from her and everybody there had been clutching the person next to them. Nobody had known, but Zee had wanted to jump into the grave with him.

Then came the prayers, which she had heard chanted so many times on 'Songs of Praise'. Familiar and anonymous as the whine of a power tool. The prayers had drilled holes in her brain somehow, sawn through her stomach. At the end, when the prayers stopped, there had been trumpets. A policeman with polished buttons and white gloves had played the Last Post. Then they had all left the graveyard and eaten neat little ham sandwiches at the funeral tea. People had talked, one or two of them had even laughed. They had left her dad all alone in a cold dark hole in the ground, and had a party.

For days afterwards she had not felt right. As if they had done DIY on her body and not put the bits back together again. Slashed to pieces on the inside she had felt.

Grieving had been just too hard so she had stopped grieving. She had concentrated on schoolwork. She would sit her GCSEs, then her A levels, then she would get out and away – that was the plan. But with Conor the plan had wavered and now Conor had left her too. She had seen it in his eyes the moment he saw her face. Her face...

Grief consumed her with a roar and she burrowed deep in the pillows so that no one would hear her.

'*It comes at me suddenly like a wild animal,*' her mum

had said weeks ago, pulling off the dual carriageway, and Zee had wondered why, if she saw it coming, she couldn't just avoid it altogether.

She understood better now because it came at her, too, like an animal, like a tiger from a bush. The grief tiger knocked her down, shook her about, chewed her up, bit by bit, until her whole being was lost in tears. It tossed her back and forth in its huge jaws and all she could do was hang on until it had finished with her. There was no escape. Because right now, right this minute, Zee wanted her dad more than anything else in the world. Willing him to be there, begging him, she twisted around and dared to look in the window one more time.

But there was only blackness, and her crying would go on forever.

26

Miguel and Tasha, in the silver Renault, hovered at the top of the narrow street.

'You think?' he prompted.

'It does look familiar,' said Tasha half-heartedly. 'But all these streets look the same.'

'Yes, but we *will* find him.'

'Yes,' she sighed. 'Thanks, Miguel, you've been a brick.'

'A brick?' His eyes widened. 'This is good?'

'Very good,' she giggled.

Tasha knew how much she owed Miguel. Not only had he been cruising East Belfast with her for days, but he had kept her spirits up too. He turned the steering wheel and they wound slowly down between the red-brick houses. Earlier they had found the chip shop Tasha visited on the eleventh night. Ruby lived in one of the streets near it, but which one? Which house? That garage with the blue door did look familiar, she thought. In the mirror Miguel grinned at a gang of urchins who had materialised from nowhere and were racing after the car, laughing and shouting.

'Kids, they are little detectives the whole world over.'

Tasha had an idea. 'Pull in,' she said excitedly. 'We'll ask them.'

The moment Miguel stopped, the kids peered in,

some of them smearing the windows with grubby hands. When Tasha leapt out they would have run away if she hadn't stopped them

'Wait! Please wait!' She glanced at two women standing in a doorway with their arms crossed, staring at her suspiciously. Three men leaning against a wall undressed her with their eyes. Tasha decided that the children were definitely her best bet.

'I'm looking for Ruby Mason,' she told them. 'I'll give a pound to whoever tells me where she lives.'

'Are ye police?' one demanded.

'I'm a friend of hers.' Some of them laughed at this and others stared doubtfully but Tasha's spirits soared. At least they seemed to know Ruby. Had she really, after days of searching, found the right street at last?

'Bet she's a loan shark,' muttered a boy of about ten.

'I most certainly am not,' said Tasha indignantly.

'She's English so she is!'

'She's dead posh!'

'Who are ye?'

'I've told you – I'm a friend of Ruby's.'

One of them, slightly older than the others, looked at her shrewdly. 'So how come ye don't know where she lives then?'

Nothing she said was going to be believed. Round here even tiny kids knew better than to give information to strangers.

'I'll tell you what,' she said, 'a pound to whoever tells Ruby that Tasha is here to see her.'

That did the trick. They hurtled off and disappeared

around the corner at the end of the street. A moment later she heard them again, racing along the back alley behind the houses facing her. Then a door opened just yards away and Ruby poked her face out cautiously.

'At last!' Tasha hurried towards her in delight, leaving Miguel with the car.

'It really is ye! This'll kick-start the rumour industry round here.'

'Will it? Oh dear, I'm sorry.'

'That's a'right.' Ruby fluffed her hair up theatrically with the flat of her hand. 'I'll tell them all I'm being interviewed by a journalist from *Cosmo* magazine. Sure me street cred'll shoot through the ozone layer.'

It dawned on Tasha that Ruby was mocking herself, and she grinned back at her.

'How did ye find me?' asked Ruby.

'It's taken days. No one helped us – that's for sure.'

'Don't take it personally. Round here folk look out for each other.'

'I remembered from the eleventh night that you lived in this district – in a street with King Billy painted on the gable.'

'That helped, did it?' Ruby threw back her head and laughed, her big earrings jangling.

'I didn't realise quite how many King Billys there are around here,' admitted Tasha.

'Good on ye! Ye must have been at it for days, so you must. I daresay you've a good reason, Tasha?'

'I'm looking for Gary.'

'I thought ye might be. Sorry, he's not here.'

'But I was sure he would be.' Tasha felt like bursting into tears. 'I was counting on it! I don't know where else to look for him.'

'Why d'ye want him?'

'I've got a message from Zee.'

Ruby's face crinkled sorrowfully. 'That poor kid. How's she doin'?'

'Better than she was. I'm going to take care of her now. Zee's leaving Belfast and she's moving to England with me.'

'Leavin'?' Ruby's forehead folded in a frown. 'Oh my, we didn't expect that.'

'*We*?' pounced Tasha. 'So you do know where Gary is!'

'I . . . could give him a message if ye like.'

'No, I need to talk to him myself.' Tasha was surprised by her own firmness and she added, 'Come on! I owe them both that much.'

Ruby studied her for a moment, then she nodded towards Miguel and the silver Renault. 'It's some distance. Can we take the car?'

'Of course we can.'

'I want to stop on the way though – to buy flowers.'

Ruby bought carnations, a big multi-coloured bunch of them. Tasha didn't understand why until they pulled up at the big wrought iron gates of a cemetery.

'Gary's here?' she asked, taken aback. 'Not . . . not . . . ?'

'Nah! He's visitin' his da's grave. He keeps it nice so he does – he even planted flowers on it last year.'

252

'Really?'

'Yeah, primroses – nicked them from the railway line, wouldn't ye know? I warned him it's against the law but ye know Gary.'

No, thought Tasha. She might have had sex with Gary but she was starting to realise that she did not know him at all. They set off through the cemetery with Miguel beside them. It was a huge place, like a city of the dead with graves stretching right up a hill into the distance. Ruby seemed to know exactly where she was going though and she led them expertly along a maze of winding paths.

It was the colours that surprised Tasha. The colours of thousands of flowers. Scarlets and ochres, oceans of blues and greens, acres of heathery purples – all the colours of the rainbow spilling from hundreds of caskets that decorated gravestones. There were cut flowers and artificial ones, paper, nylon and silk. Windmills had even been pushed into some of the graves, gaudy little children's windmills which whirled around, clicking busily. A high breeze bounced about their heads as they walked, blowing rosy scents.

Tasha was amazed. If she thought about the dead at all, she thought of them as well and truly gone. But this cemetery felt different. As if the dead were still around somehow, as if they had just slipped into another room and still had to be cared for, entertained even. All this movement, all this colour...

'Ga-ry!' Ruby had cupped her hands around her mouth and yelled.

When he turned round, Tasha blushed. How, after all that had happened, could Gary still do that to her? Was it fear or excitement or some weird mixture of both? Not that it mattered now. Whatever had been between them, whatever could have been, was lost.

'Hello, Gary,' she said wearily, 'I've been chasing after you for days.'

'I've been chasing you for weeks,' said Gary. 'Never thought I'd catch up with you here though.'

'It is good to find you,' said Miguel. 'Hello again.' He offered Gary his hand but Gary just stared at him. Tasha knew he was remembering how Miguel had thrown him out of the house the last time they met.

'Don't blame Ruby,' said Tasha. 'I made her bring us here.'

'Nobody's ever *made* Ruby do anything in her whole life,' Gary replied. 'Sure that's why we're friends.'

Ruby was busy putting her carnations on the grave but she smiled up at him. 'Ye've got this looking gorgeous,' she said, pointing at a posy of sweet peas and the white stones that formed a border round the grave.

'Yes,' said Miguel. 'It is good to have a grave.'

Tasha wondered what he meant exactly but before she could ask Miguel began reading the inscription on the headstone. She began to wish that he had stayed in the car.

Sergeant Jack Proctor
11th February 1961 to 6th June 2002
Killed by terrorists

'Your father died the month I left Bosnia,' he told them.

'So?' said Gary rudely. 'You wanted to come here, didn't you?'

'Of course not. But there was nothing left for me in Bosnia.'

'So you came to Britain for a better life?'

'I had very nice life, thank you. I was Head of Music at a High School in Sarajevo. Nice house, nice car, nice friends.'

Ruby frowned. 'What happened, then, Miguel?'

'The war happened. It is a long story.' Miguel sighed heavily. 'First there were shortages – short of petrol, of equipment, short of food. Soon neighbour turned upon neighbour, Christian on Muslim, Muslim on Christian too.'

'I remember it,' said Ruby unexpectedly. 'I saw pictures on the telly. Whole streets got burned out, loadsa people died there, didn't they?' Miguel nodded and Ruby's voice continued, soft and warm and interested, not embarrassed at all. 'Did ye have family die there?'

'Yes, my parents first and then my wife.'

'No,' gasped Tasha. 'No!'

'In the blockade of Sarajevo no medicine came into the city, no food. My parents were old and died because of this. My wife – a sniper killed her.'

'You had a wife . . . ?' Tasha had been so wrapped up in herself, she had never thought about Miguel's past life. She had never even thought of him having a real life. She almost cringed with shame. How could she have been so selfish?

'That's hellish, Miguel,' said Ruby and she reached out and rubbed his big hands between her own, as natural and caring as a mother.

Gary cleared his throat and when he spoke he did not sound quite so hostile. 'What did you do after your wife died?'

'At first I had no wish to go on. But then I realised – if I give up and die they have killed me too. One more dead Bosnian.'

'But you musta wanted to pay them back?'

'Yes, I did. But if I spend my whole life angry, I will destroy myself too. I will become just like them.'

'So what *did* you do? How did you get over it?'

'You never get over it. But is important to learn from it.'

'Yeah?' Gary was staring at him. 'What did you learn?'

'That people must stop hating each other. They must stop. Now I help refugees to settle – this is more useful than fighting. I have music too,' he added. 'My anger, sadness, my pain are all in my music. Perhaps when people hear me play they will understand how terrible war is. And one day maybe there will be no more war.'

Gary scoffed, 'No more war?' He pointed at his father's gravestone. 'Look at him. They shot him at point-blank range – that's what it said on the news that night. Know what point-blank means, Tasha?'

'Gary—' warned Ruby.

Gary's voice shook. 'I answered the door that night, *I* let them in.'

256

'You were a child,' said Miguel.

'Do you think that helps? It doesn't – it never did. Anyway, look at me now.' He banged himself on the chest. 'All grown up and just as useless as I was that night.'

'Pah!' Miguel spoke sharply. 'How you behave now is up to you.'

'We can't all just walk away,' said Gary hotly. 'I wanted to give these guys what they deserved – bullets.'

'You have seen how revenge turns to madness.' Miguel was shouting back. 'Your sister is in hospital, is she not?'

'It's all right for you! You're working with refugees and you're a musical genius. I'm tone deaf for God's sake!' Gary scowled. 'What could a useless sod like me do?'

'Stop wallowing in self pity. This would be a start. If you don't you will be destroyed – you and your family too.'

Silence descended on them all. Only the wind made a noise, buffeting the sweet petals of flowers which danced like confetti across the cemetery. The windmills whirled even faster and somewhere, wind-chimes tinkled. Ruby wandered off and Miguel followed her.

Quietly, awkwardly, Tasha passed on Zee's message. Gary barely blinked.

'Don't you understand?' she pressed. 'Zee's leaving Ireland. We're both leaving.'

'Maybe it's for the best,' he said. 'Tash, about that night in the field – I was a pig and I'm sorry.'

Tasha surprised herself again. 'It wasn't all your fault. I was hellbent on romance this summer.'

'It wasn't exactly romantic, was it?'

'Our first night was. Do you remember? The big bonfire, the backstreets, those fish and chips.'

His eyes twinkled unexpectedly. 'I've never heard anyone call a chip supper romantic before. Who says posh girls are hard to please?'

'I'd have done anything for you after that night, Gary.'

'And I still managed to blow it.' He stroked her cheek gently and the thrill of it sizzled all the way down to her knees. Tasha caught his hand quickly.

'Do one thing for me, Gary?'

'What?'

'Visit Zee before she leaves.'

'I don't think so. Zee's better off forgetting I exist.'

'How can she?'

But Gary had stopped listening. He was bending down now, pulling a pink carnation out of the bunch that Ruby had brought his father. Tasha could see Ruby a little way off, kneeling by another grave. For some reason, Miguel was kneeling too. With a jolt she realised they were praying.

She followed Gary across the graves and joined them by a clean white marble stone sculpted into the shape of a tiny angel. The inscription was in silver letters.

Here lies
Sharon Mason
Eight weeks old
Killed by a stray bullet
God have mercy on us all

Tasha cried out and clapped her hand over her mouth to stop more cries following. Tears bubbled down her face. 'I'm so sorry. Ruby, oh, Ruby...I never knew.'

'Ruby's baby and my dad,' said Gary quietly, 'were both killed in the same week. The two of us met right here.'

'We kinda took each other on,' explained Ruby.

Tasha gulped back her tears. Was there no end to people's misery? All these weeks she had thought Ruby was a rival, frivolous, stupid, and promiscuous. But it was *she* who had been all those things. What Ruby and Gary had went far deeper than that.

'Time for us to go,' said Miguel and he put his arm around her.

Tasha nodded. What a relief it was to have found Gary and finished her task, to walk away, to leave Ruby and Gary alone with all their hurt. What a relief it was to have Miguel's arm to snuggle into.

'Wait,' Gary called after them. 'Will you say goodbye to Zee for me?'

'No!' Miguel swung sharply round. 'She leaves on the boat tomorrow night. Say goodbye yourself, young man.'

27

Zee moved methodically around the room, packing a small hold-all. Her mother was bringing all her gear from home, packed into their two smartest suitcases, ready for her arrival at Redbales School. Not that the pupils would be staring at her luggage, she thought.

She looked again in the mirror which they had put back yesterday. Brave, they had called her when she looked in it. Adult, dignified, mature; the compliments had flown. Zee touched her cheek just below the eye where rows of stitches were pulled tight into a little hollow. That bit would never look the same again. Some wounds had healed already though, and others had lost their vividness. The swelling had gone down too and some of the stitches had dissolved, they no longer stood out like railway tracks. Maybe little children would not hide from her after all.

She was relieved that they were going straight to the docks. It would have been awful to face pitying neighbours and unbearable to say goodbye to her home, to her bedroom, even to that awful fountain. She would remember for ever the details of the ivy-covered cottage; every blistering flake of paint, the crannies where she had played hide-and-seek, and every dusty nook she had ever curled up in with a book. No one could take memories away.

'It's not too late to change your mind,' her mum said as soon as she arrived.

'No, thanks.' Nothing else had changed after all. Conor had not come back to visit her and Gary had not gone home. Maybe, just maybe, when she left, things would get back to normal. 'Do you want the flowers, Mum?'

'I don't feel very flowery.' Then, briskly, she added, 'I'm sure other patients would appreciate them. Now, have you thanked the nurses?'

Zee did so as she left, even the one who had stuck a needle in her, and they all wished her luck with her new life in England.

'We make our own luck,' her mum muttered as they walked down the corridor. 'Just you remember that.' But she put her arm around Zee protectively when a passer-by stared at her.

'Stop worrying, Mum, I'll be okay.'

'You'll phone me every day.'

'Of course I will,' said Zee, blinking hard.

The hospital's automatic doors slid open and Zee breathed in fresh warm summer air for the first time in nearly a week. It tasted wonderful.

'The car's just over here.'

'You've never left the twins alone? They'll have the car ruined.'

'They're not alone.'

'What? Has Gary—?'

'No.' Her mother's face sagged. 'Tasha reckons he's too ashamed to face you.'

The Citroën's door flew open and Conor jumped out.

'I wasn't expecting *you*,' said Zee, flustered.

'I told you I'd be back.'

Yes, but she had not believed him. She slid into the back seat between Conor and Josh, who began flailing a fluorescent green light sabre in her face. It would make her look like a Halloween ghoul, she thought crossly, then she realised that it didn't matter. After tonight she would never see Conor again.

'I've got the front seat,' yelled Gemma in glee.

'It's mine on the way back,' declared Josh.

'Thanks for coming, Con,' she said awkwardly, though he could hardly hear her over the twins.

'I'm sorry about last time I visited, Zee. I really messed up. Things happened so fast...'

'You're here now, Con, that's what matters. I'll write to you, I promise.'

'Yeah, sure, great.'

She rested her head against his shoulder, absorbing the city for the last time as they threaded their way through the streets. Rattling across the cobbles by the docks she remembered the last time she and Conor had been there together. Remembered the excitement of his arms around her, the softness of his eyes, that moment when he told her that he had loved her for ever.

Conor must have been remembering it too because he nuzzled against her head and whispered so softly that nobody else could possibly hear, 'I love you, Zee.'

'They're snogging!' exclaimed Josh in disgust.

'Shut up,' snapped his mother and Josh was so

surprised that he did. She turned the radio up loud.

Zee glanced up at Conor nervously. 'You don't have to love me,' she whispered back. 'I do understand.' Then she felt a little box being pushed into her hand.

'Maybe that's proof of a sort,' he said gruffly. 'You seem to need it.'

She looked down at the brown paper bag. 'Is it a ring?'

'Not exactly.'

She started opening it but Conor restrained her hastily. 'Not here!'

'Okay, but I promise I'll write when I do.'

He kissed her gently on her nose. 'You're special, Zee, you do know that? You always will be.'

They sat in silence after that and, judging by the tightness of his hand, Conor felt just as choked up as she did. When they drew up opposite the ferry, its bows were gaping and it was swallowing up cars, one by one. A red funnel puffed impatiently and lights shone in cabin portholes. So many times Zee had seen the boat like this, straining to be off and so many times she had wished that she was on it. But now...

'Off you go,' said her mum. She gave Zee the briefest brush of a kiss, and then, when Zee had hugged the twins, hurried them straight back into the car. Zee had never seen her so business-like but she was glad. Tearful goodbyes were awful. 'Go!' said her mum again, gruffly, and turned the radio up even louder.

Zee didn't look back. Conor carried her luggage across the concrete apron, then Tasha appeared at the top of the gangway, waving wildly. Magda and Miguel were up there with her, seeing her safely aboard. Zee took one last lingering look around.

'I thought ... just maybe ... '

Conor read her mind. 'You thought Gary might turn up? No chance. He's far too big a coward.'

'Is that so, sunshine?' came Gary's voice, stung.

Zee spun round as he emerged, half pushed it seemed, from the shadows. 'Gary, it is you!'

Behind him she could make out Ruby's flouncing skirt and flying hair, but Ruby hung back as Gary approached them.

'How you doing, sis?' he asked awkwardly.

'Fine, I'm fine!' It sounded stupid the moment it left her lips.

'Jee-zus,' he said slowly and shock waves rippled across his face. For one moment Zee thought he was going to bolt again but he didn't; he stayed right there staring at her.

'I'm sorry, Zee, I'm *so* sorry ... that's what I've come to say.'

'I know you are, Gary – I've known it all along. It's all right – really it is.'

'How can you say that? It's not all right at all!'

Zee didn't know what else to say. She was just glad that he had made it, glad she would not have to leave Ireland with this huge rift still between them.

'I've no excuses,' he went on. 'I was so angry I couldn't see the half of what was going on. Couldn't see what Des Gordon was up to for a start. And I'd no idea about you and *him* ... ' He nodded abruptly at Conor. 'Even when you came after me that night, O'Keefe, I never guessed the truth. Too busy feeling sorry for myself I suppose...'

'You've been blind angry, Gary, because of Dad. 'Cos of what happened to him. I miss Dad too, you know.' Zee didn't understand exactly why she said that, it just seemed important to tell him.

'You never said so, Zee.'

'I couldn't. I couldn't talk about Dad at all. I couldn't even think about him. If I did I got stuck – *so stuck* – on that night it happened. And then I couldn't cope at all.'

'And I couldn't stop talking about him.' Gary grinned. 'I must have driven you mad...d'you reckon Dad's turning in his grave at the pair of us?'

Zee uttered something between a laugh and a cry. 'Turning? Spinning more like!'

Footsteps clattered over the cobblestones towards them. 'We couldn't just stay in the car,' came their mother's voice breathlessly and there she was, standing behind them with the twins. 'Don't forget the good memories too,' she said. 'The family picnics, the swimming trips, blackberrying Sundays, Dad coming home on a Friday night with a fistful of chocolate bars.'

'I do remember those,' said Zee, surprising herself. She wondered how she could possibly have forgotten.

'It's what he'd want you to remember. How he lived – not how he died.'

The boat's hooter blew urgently and Zee looked at Tasha waiting at the top of the gangway. The twins started heaving her luggage about. They were all waiting for her to go. It was time to leave.

'So,' she said, 'what now, Gary? Will you go back home with Mum?'

'I will,' he said, slowly and carefully, 'if *you* will.'

'That's not fair!'

'Isn't it?' His eyes were shrewd, cutting through her façade. 'I think you want to,' he said.

She threw a glance at Conor. Would it be fair on him if she stayed? He shouldn't feel tied to a girl with a face like hers. His little box was still in her hand and on impulse she tore off the tape and squinted inside the paper bag.

'No!' exclaimed Conor but it was too late.

Condoms, a box of three. Zee burst out laughing. 'How romantic, Con!'

'It was just to show you...er...I still want...er...' He had turned bright red.

'I might not get any prettier than this,' she warned him.

'So? I might stay an arrogant git for ever.'

'I'd bet on it,' muttered Gary.

Zee hesitated. Gary wasn't the only one who could make conditions, she thought. 'I suppose I could stay,' she said, 'if the two of you were to make up.'

Gary and Conor sized each other up, a bit like they had on the eleventh night. Only this time Gary wasn't spoiling for a fight and Conor wasn't looking as if he was surrounded by aliens. In the end it was Gary who held out his hand. Conor didn't exactly shake it, more of a slap really, but the tension between them vanished.

'They're coming home,' shouted Josh excitedly, 'we're gonna be a family again!'

At that, Tasha came down the gangplank. 'You're not coming to my dad's or to Redbales, are you, Zee?' She couldn't keep the disappointment out of her voice.

'One day, maybe I will go to England,' said Zee, 'but not now.'

They fell into each other's arms and hugged tightly, too choked up to speak.

'It's been the most amazing summer,' said Tasha at last. 'We've been through so much together – I feel like a different person.'

'It's been pretty amazing for me too, Tash. You will come back for Christmas, won't you?'

'Nothing could stop me.' Tasha blinked hard. 'You're the best friend I've ever had, Zee.'

'Friends forever – yeah?'

'Forever.'

Tasha spun on her heel and fled back to the boat, and Zee leaned into the comforting, familiar form of her mother. One thing had become completely clear to her. She didn't want London or Redbales. Right now she didn't want any folk or any country except her own. She wanted to be here in Belfast with *her* family, *her* school and *her* boyfriend.

Nothing could scare her now. She had met the Grief Tiger head on after all, and she had survived. There was nothing to run away from. The tiger might still leap out at her occasionally, she knew that, but she would cope. She had got her family back.

Gemma sighed and slipped her hand happily through Zee's. 'I won't get to see those furry guards,' she said and then she beamed at Josh. 'And *you* won't get the front seat home.'

Gary pulled Ruby out of the shadows and Magda and Miguel joined them. With a series of farewell hoots, the boat pulled away and Conor put his arms around Zee and kissed her.

She turned and looked at the two suitcases stranded on the pier and at the car a hundred yards away, and then she grinned at Ruby. 'Do you think these big lads are expecting me to lug my cases all the way back there?'

'Wi' guys, nothin' surprises me,' said Ruby, twinkling. 'We'll have to keep these two in order, so we will.'

Zee turned to them with her hands on her hips and a voice that would brook no argument. 'Right, come on then, you big eejits! One case each!'

Conor looked at Gary and shook his head solemnly. 'Bossy as ever, isn't she?'

'Aye, we don't stand a chance,' said Gary. 'Know what I think, Con? I think you and me had best stick together.'